LOVE AND THE G...

The Duke had brought with him the lantern that he always kept in his cabin. He had used it in the past when he had sometimes gone ashore alone at night.

Now, without speaking to Jenkins, he lit the lantern and then, moving a little further into the cave, he lifted the lantern high and saw exactly all that the King had told him he would find.

On either side of the cave, which did not go in very far, there were a number of large rocks.

They did not quite reach the roof of the cave, but left just enough space, he thought, to hold the statue of Apollo invisible to a casual explorer.

Jenkins was watching him and, when the Duke put down his lantern, he knew exactly what to do without any instructions.

Together they went back, lifted the statue very very carefully and carried it into the cave.

They placed it gently on top of the rough rocks and there was then no more than six inches between the statue of Apollo and the roof of the cave.

The Duke was thankful to find that the rocks were dry and so there was no likelihood of the sea flooding in and sweeping the precious statue away.

As he laid Apollo gently down, now back at last on his own land, the Duke experienced a strange feeling.

Something he had never felt before.

He could not explain it.

THE BARBARA CARTLAND
PINK COLLECTION

Titles in this series

LOVE AND THE GODS

BARBARA CARTLAND

Barbaracartland.com Ltd

Copyright © 2012 by Cartland Promotions
First published on the internet in August 2012
by Barbaracartland.com Ltd

ISBN 978-1-908411-84-6

Printed and bound in Great Britain
by Mimeo of Huntingdon, Cambridgeshire.

THE BARBARA CARTLAND PINK COLLECTION

Dame Barbara Cartland is still regarded as the most prolific bestselling author in the history of the world.

In her lifetime she was frequently in the Guinness Book of Records for writing more books than any other living author.

Her most amazing literary feat was to double her output from 10 books a year to over 20 books a year when she was 77 to meet the huge demand.

She went on writing continuously at this rate for 20 years and wrote her very last book at the age of 97, thus completing an incredible 400 books between the ages of 77 and 97.

Her publishers finally could not keep up with this phenomenal output, so at her death in 2000 she left behind an amazing 160 unpublished manuscripts, something that no other author has ever achieved.

Barbara's son, Ian McCorquodale, together with his daughter Iona, felt that it was their sacred duty to publish all these titles for Barbara's millions of admirers all over the world who so love her wonderful romances.

So in 2004 they started publishing the 160 brand new Barbara Cartlands as *The Barbara Cartland Pink Collection*, as Barbara's favourite colour was always pink – and yet more pink!

The Barbara Cartland Pink Collection is published monthly exclusively by Barbaracartland.com and the books are numbered in sequence from 1 to 160.

Enjoy receiving a brand new Barbara Cartland book each month by taking out an annual subscription to the Pink Collection, or purchase the books individually.

The Pink Collection is available from the Barbara Cartland website www.barbaracartland.com via mail order and through all good bookshops.

In addition Ian and Iona are proud to announce that The Barbara Cartland Pink Collection is now available in ebook format as from Valentine's Day 2011.

For more information, please contact us at:

Barbaracartland.com Ltd.
Camfield Place
Hatfield
Hertfordshire AL9 6JE
United Kingdom

Telephone: +44 (0)1707 642629
Fax: +44 (0)1707 663041
Email: info@barbaracartland.com

THE LATE DAME BARBARA CARTLAND

Barbara Cartland who sadly died in May 2000 at the age of nearly 99 was the world's most famous romantic novelist who wrote 723 books in her lifetime with worldwide sales of over 1 billion copies and her books were translated into 36 different languages.

As well as romantic novels, she wrote historical biographies, 6 autobiographies, theatrical plays, books of advice on life, love, vitamins and cookery. She also found time to be a political speaker and television and radio personality.

She wrote her first book at the age of 21 and this was called *Jigsaw*. It became an immediate bestseller and sold 100,000 copies in hardback and was translated into 6 different languages. She wrote continuously throughout her life, writing bestsellers for an astonishing 76 years. Her books have always been immensely popular in the United States, where in 1976 her current books were at numbers 1 & 2 in the B. Dalton bestsellers list, a feat never achieved before or since by any author.

Barbara Cartland became a legend in her own lifetime and will be best remembered for her wonderful romantic novels, so loved by her millions of readers throughout the world.

Her books will always be treasured for their moral message, her pure and innocent heroines, her good looking and dashing heroes and above all her belief that the power of love is more important than anything else in everyone's life.

*"When you fall in love, you touch Heaven –
and Heaven touches you."*

Barbara Cartland

CHAPTER ONE
1870

The Duke of Sherbourne finished dressing and then called out to his valet,

"Did you remember to tell the grooms I wanted to drive my new team of horses today, Jenkins?"

"They'll be round as soon as Your Grace's finished breakfast," the valet replied.

"I am looking forward to trying them out. When I bought them from their previous owner, he told me they were the fastest team he had ever handled."

Jenkins, who was used to the Duke talking to him while he was dressing, merely nodded.

He knew that his Master was noted as one of the best drivers in London and that his stables were filled with horses that were the envy of every man.

"I suppose I am dining out tonight, Jenkins?" the Duke enquired.

"Yes, Your Grace."

Jenkins walked towards the writing table that stood in the corner of the Duke's bedroom and glanced down at the book lying open on it.

He knew only too well that his Master would forget the engagements he had every night and therefore he was always ready to answer this question by looking in the diary before he called the Duke.

"Tonight Your Grace be dining out at Marlborough House with His Royal Highness the Prince of Wales."

"Indeed I am. It's a most important occasion as he wants me to meet some new friends who have just arrived in London."

He turned round to face Jenkins.

"For goodness sake, Jenkins, see that I am on time, and don't forget the present I have for the Princess, whose birthday it is tomorrow."

"It be packed up and ready for Your Grace. Mr. Simmonds brought the coloured paper Your Grace wished it to be wrapped in."

Mr. Simmonds was the Duke's private secretary and he was adept at carrying out punctiliously any order given to him.

The Duke seemed satisfied and walked towards the door and Jenkins hurried after him to make sure he had put a handkerchief in his coat pocket. To his relief he saw he had not forgotten and it was just peeping out at the top.

The Duke walked down the corridor towards the top of the staircase.

Sherbourne House was one of the largest and most prestigious houses in Park Lane.

Everyone who served His Grace was well aware that once the horses were seen waiting outside with his new and up-to-date chaise, a small crowd would invariably gather to watch him drive off.

It was not surprising that people were interested.

The footmen rolling down the red carpet over the steps from the front door were wearing the full Sherbourne livery. It was not only stylish but very colourful.

The butler was waiting at the top of the steps to see the Duke off and he was naturally smarter than any servant in real life or on the stage.

The Duke himself was a hero to every man who was keen on racing, as his horses regularly won the Classic races. He, therefore, had the admiration and respect of the crowds whenever he appeared on a Racecourse.

Now two more passers-by joined the small crowd that had collected outside the house as soon as the horses and the Duke's chaise drove into view.

They had almost instinctively stopped to admire the thoroughbreds and they knew their owner would appear in a few minutes.

In Hyde Park, which the Duke's house faced, there were already people walking across from under the trees, as they wanted to see what was happening on the other side of the road.

When the Duke appeared in the doorway, a murmur came from the lips of those waiting.

The women, if they dared, would have applauded his appearance.

He certainly looked exceedingly smart and he was undoubtedly one of the most handsome men they had ever seen.

His dark, almost black hair, was brushed back from a square forehead and his features were classical.

At the same time he had a smile that most women found irresistible.

Holding his tall hat in his right hand, that had just been given to him by one of the footmen, he stood gazing at his horses.

He was thinking that they were the best buy he had ever made, all pitch black except for a white star on their foreheads and a faint touch of white on their back fetlocks – they were not only unusual but magnificent.

The Duke put on his hat and started to walk down the steps.

As he did so, the crowd pressed themselves even closer against the gold-tipped railings and the children put their hands through them to point at the horses.

They were waiting there as excited and expectant as their elders to see the team drive off.

Without hurrying, the Duke seated himself in the driving seat and picked up the reins.

The groom accompanying him then jumped into the small seat at the back of the chaise and, as the butler and four footmen bowed, His Grace moved off.

Instinctively, as if they could not stop themselves, the crowd now cheered and clapped.

The chaise reached the gate and the horses passed through it and the crowd cheered again.

By this time, more people coming up the street had increased the crowd and the Duke raised his hat to them as he passed and they cheered him again.

Then he was moving with an experienced hand through the traffic and, when he reached Hyde Park Corner, he turned right.

By now he had settled down to enjoy the long drive to Windsor Castle that lay ahead of him.

Only when he was out of London and leaving the houses behind him did the Duke begin to wonder again, as he had when he had received the letter last night, why Her Majesty Queen Victoria had asked for him.

He had been at Windsor Castle only a week ago, as he had been running two of his best racehorses at Ascot.

Out of politeness he had called on Her Majesty and she had been delighted to see him.

Yet, after they had talked on various subjects, she had not appeared to want him to do anything at all special for her.

Therefore this sudden summons to come as soon as possible to Windsor Castle had been a surprise.

He was always welcome there because Her Majesty liked to have young and handsome men around her and the Duke in particular was one of her favourites.

But he had the feeling when he read the letter Her Majesty's secretary had written to him that she was going to ask him to undertake a special task for her.

What it could be he had no idea, but he decided it was a waste of time to speculate.

So he concentrated on driving his horses once they were out of the London traffic more quickly than he had ever driven before.

'Oswald was right,' he told himself, 'when he said these were the best horseflesh he had ever possessed. I am sure he will miss them.'

He could understand that his friend Lord Longlow had been reluctant to part with such an outstanding team and the Duke had felt it was almost cruel to take them from him.

But he had learnt that Lord Longlow's eldest son had run up a huge gambling debt and it was a question of parting either with the horses or with some of his collection of pictures and these he prized even more than his stable.

He had asked a considerable sum for the horses because he needed the money and the Duke had paid him willingly – not only because what he was now buying was exceptional but because he was fond of their owner and was glad to help him.

He thought that his son had behaved disgracefully and not for the first time.

It merely made him repeat what he had said so often, not just to himself but aloud, that he was glad he was not married.

'I have no intention of marrying,' he told himself now as the horses were moving even faster, 'and it will be no use Grandmama, when she comes to stay tomorrow, wasting so much time, when we might be talking about the past, begging me to take a wife.'

He was now twenty-seven and his family had a long time ago decided it was essential that he should marry and provide an heir to his ancient title, his vast estates and his incredibly valuable possessions.

The Duke had been an only son and there was no near relative to inherit.

Yet, although he had no intention of dying if he could help it, the family invariably behaved as if he would soon pass away and there would be no one to take his place, or rather, as they thought of it – 'his throne'.

Of course the Head of the Family, and it was quite a large one, was of tremendous stature.

The Sherbournes had played a significant role in the history of England ever since the reign of Henry I.

The Duke assured them all that he had no intention of dying for the time being and equally he had no intention of marrying.

He had no wish to be tied down to one woman, as he expressed it so vividly, and he wished to enjoy himself and continue to play the field.

It was not at all surprising that quite a number of beautiful women had already lost their hearts to the Duke.

And he had said to his grandmother the last time she had stayed with him that he had no intention yet of settling down and he would not take a wife until he met the right person.

"How can you talk like that, dearest David?" his grandmother had asked. "From what I hear, every young unmarried girl in London is at your feet."

6

"If you said, 'is gazing at my strawberry leaves', you would be more correct," the Duke replied sarcastically. "As you know, Grandmama, the ambition of every young girl is to be a Duchess."

He paused before he added sharply,

"But I have no intention of marrying some giggling little *debutante* who wants to capture me as a prize with which to impress her contemporaries!"

"Really, David, you do talk nonsense. Of course women want to marry you for yourself and not entirely for your title."

The Duke forced himself not to interrupt as she battled on,

"At the same time, if a girl is really beautiful, as your mother was and comes from a reasonably suitable family, it is exactly who you require in a wife and we will welcome her with open arms."

"I realise that, but as you well know, Grandmama, I find it difficult to be attached to one woman for any length of time."

He saw that she was about to argue with him and so he carried on hastily,

"Shall I say that I enjoy the pursuit, in the same way as I enjoy watching one of my horses race. But once it has passed the winning post, then I begin to think of what will be the next race to interest me."

His grandmother looked exasperated.

"You know as well as I do, dearest, that you have to marry someone. I do think it is time you took life more seriously and more important than anything else provide us with an heir to the Dukedom."

"I quite understand what you want, Grandmama, but remember that it is I who will have to live with the much acclaimed Duchess!"

He sighed.

"I find that women after only a short acquaintance invariably repeat themselves endlessly and tell me stories I have heard before. Then, although I know I should not say it, frankly they become unspeakably boring."

His grandmother had flung up her hands.

"Really, David, you are impossible! How can you have been bored with Lady Emma who was, I thought, one of the loveliest girls I have ever seen?"

"I agree with you there, but apart from her beauty she has nothing to say and the last time I dined with her I yawned the hours away."

He wanted to make his grandmother laugh, but she just wrinkled her nose.

"You are really impossible, David," she repeated. "The trouble is that you are regrettably far too clever for the average woman, but it is essential for you to be married even if you don't settle down."

The Duke did not continue the conversation, simply because he had heard it so often and found it tedious.

Instead he insisted on taking his grandmother to see the latest objects he had collected on a journey to Africa and she had to admit they were unusual and interesting additions to his other treasures.

He had followed the example of his ancestors, who had collected not only pictures and furniture but objects of historical interest.

His house in Park Lane and his castle in the country were the envy of all his contemporaries, as, when he had inherited the title, he found numerous treasures that had been passed down through the ages by his ancestors and he had seen none of them before.

He did not want people to envy him or to applaud his purchases and thus he only showed his most recent acquisitions to the more intelligent members of his family.

After his grandmother had stopped pleading with him to marry, she had been enchanted with some exquisite carvings and strange weapons over three hundred years old.

"I cannot think, David," she said, "how you were clever enough to find these fascinating objects."

"I think the right answer to that, Grandmama," the Duke replied, "is that I take infinite trouble, as few others do, to learn the language of the people I meet in parts of the world where the usual sightseer never ventures."

"I well remember," she smiled, "as a little boy you talked with a French maid I had. She was so thrilled when you asked her in French to tell you what she was doing and for the French word for everything you took to her."

"She was very helpful to me," the Duke answered, "just as I have found other women in many parts of the world who were only too willing to assist when I wished to learn their language."

"And of course to make love," she grinned at him. "Although I would hate you to marry a foreigner, if she is pretty and clever, I would be only too happy to accept her."

The Duke laughed.

"I am afraid, Grandmama, the women I have learnt from and found to be the best teachers, were old and their appearance was not of any particular note."

He paused before he added,

"What I was making use of was their brains that at the time were of more interest to me than anything else."

His grandmother threw up her hands again.

The Duke knew it was with difficulty she prevented herself from arguing with him, as she was well aware that most of the marriageable ladies in the Social world they lived in were not particularly noted for their brains.

She left him, after begging him once again to take a bride.

The Duke then walked into his library and looked round at the numerous volumes, many of which he had collected himself.

He thought that if only they could live and breathe he would be only too glad to ask them all to be his wife!

He knew so well what the conversation would be tomorrow evening when he was dining alone with one of the most admired women in the *Beau Monde*.

She would undoubtedly flirt with him with a charm that could not be equalled even by the French.

They would talk of love as it concerned them both and she would undoubtedly flatter him because he was so handsome.

After that, they would talk about her and about her exquisite beauty and pulsating body until the dawn came.

Then he would walk home.

Unlike most of his contemporaries the Duke did not on these occasions keep his carriage waiting for him round the corner.

Even if the lady's house was some distance from Park Lane, he always walked home.

He felt he needed to blow away the hours they had spent together and he wanted to start a new day as the stars began to flicker out and the first rays of the sun rose in the Eastern sky.

The moment when the darkness vanished and the day began again convinced him more than anything else that all he had just experienced was just a passing fancy and that there was a great deal more to come of which he was not yet aware.

It was the expectation of the next day that to him made life exciting.

Far too many people, he had often thought, lived in the past, thought in the past, remembering only the past.

For him it had always been the future, the surprise and excitement of the unknown and the thrill of finding something new, something he had not seen before.

Inevitably, like the passing of one day into another, and one night into day, it was tomorrow that counted and he quickly forgot yesterday.

He knew this as surely as if he listened to a voice that came from inside his brain.

Whatever his relatives may say and however much his grandmother might plead with him, it was what lay ahead that mattered.

What he had not yet experienced in life made him even more determined than ever not to marry.

'There is still so much of the world I have not seen and so many beautiful women I have yet not met,' he told himself, 'and I must be free to seek the unknown.'

Finally, he would go to sleep in his own bed with the first light of the day creeping up on the horizon.

*

As the Duke drove on, he was not thinking of his grandmother's pleadings but of what he might find waiting for him at Windsor Castle.

Her Majesty's urgent message might easily prove to be nothing of any real consequence.

Yet his instinct told him that she needed him for something unusual that he could not even guess at.

'I am just being over-imaginative,' he mused as he passed through a village. 'There was nothing new at Windsor

11

Castle when I was last there, except for one Lady-in-Waiting who was definitely younger and prettier than the rest!'

He thought, if he was asked to stay on for dinner, he might see if she was as entrancing as she looked.

However, perhaps she would be as dull as most of the others were – he had known them for too long to expect anything but the usual banal conversation.

It could become more interesting when there were foreigners visiting Her Majesty, especially if they came from a country he had not yet visited or he had very little knowledge about.

Because he had travelled so much, such countries were becoming fewer every year.

Nevertheless, on his last visit to Windsor Castle he had met a man from the Balkans, who had travelled a great deal in Asia and the Duke had found that what he told him was different from anything he had known previously.

In fact, the conversation had been so interesting he had almost set out for Asia as soon as he returned home.

Then he told himself that he was sure there were other places of great interest.

He had not wished to be involved in the diplomatic warfare that was currently taking place between Russia and Great Britain.

There was no disguising on whose side the Queen was and she spoke angrily and contemptuously about the Russians. She was furious at their behaviour in attempting to make the Balkans part of the Russian Empire.

'There are already too many engaged in trying to prevent what they are doing,' the Duke thought, 'for me to take any part in it.'

He had then forced himself to be more interested in North America than he had been previously.

Yet now, as he neared Windsor Castle, he had an uncomfortable feeling.

It was that Her Majesty was going to persuade him to become involved in her confrontation with the Czar.

The Duke, when he left school, had for some years been in the Army and his family had in consequence been terrified that he might be killed in action, as there was no close relative to take his place.

It was after he had served in three campaigns that he had been persuaded to pay more attention to his estates and that naturally included his many thoroughbreds and the beautiful women who pursued him.

He had enjoyed his years in the Army and yet he was now finding that, unless there was someone especially interesting for him to meet, he was bored.

The daily round of amusements in the Social world was invariably a repetition of what had occurred yesterday, the day before and the day before that.

Even the women he made love to talked to him in the same way as the one before, and the one before that, had done.

'I must think of something new to do,' the Duke reflected as he passed through Eton and across the river.

Now he was in the town of Windsor and The Castle was just ahead of him.

For a moment his thoughts seemed to soar into the air.

He had a distinct feeling that the sky was opening for him on a new and exciting project – something he had never done before.

Then he laughed at himself.

Everything was just as it had always been.

There was nothing new about the sentries standing at the gates or the imposing castle itself.

'I am not stepping forth into a new tomorrow,' he thought sadly, 'but merely looking back on what I saw and heard yesterday and the day before.'

The door was opened by a servant, who smiled at him and whom he knew by name and then an equerry appeared who had obviously been waiting for him.

He was a young man and the Duke could not help thinking that he was wasting his time at Windsor Castle. He might have been more active in the great world outside, perhaps in a Regiment or in attendance on the Viceroy of India or on a British Ambassador to some obscure country that ordinary English people knew very little about.

That was why the Duke had enjoyed his visits to Nepal and many other places with which few of the Social world were familiar and he had visited China and found it most uncomfortable but intensely interesting.

He had been planning that he would one day go to Tibet and it was only his deep interest in his horseflesh that had prevented him from doing so.

He enjoyed, if nothing else in England, the racing that was taking place at this particular time of year and almost every day his horses were running and winning at some fashionable Racecourse.

The equerry was now taking the Duke up the stairs to Her Majesty's private apartments.

"Have you been busy since I left two weeks ago?" the Duke asked him.

The equerry smiled.

"We are always busy, as Your Grace well knows. Her Majesty always wants to hear about what is happening in other countries, so we have had endless Ambassadors coming here day after day."

"Has anything unusual happened?" the Duke asked him hopefully.

The equerry shook his head.

"Not that I am aware of. But I regret to say that they don't always tell me."

The Duke knew this to be true.

The Queen liked to keep everything to herself and especially from her eldest son, the Prince of Wales, who was longing to become involved in the affairs of State.

They reached the Queen's private apartments.

The equerry in charge bowed to the Duke.

"Her Majesty was certain you would not be long, Your Grace," he said. "She has been expecting you this last half-hour."

"I came more quickly, thanks to my new team of horses, than I have ever done before."

The equerry laughed.

"You know as well as I do, Your Grace, that Her Majesty is waiting impatiently at the end of the journey, so she inevitably thinks everyone is late even if they have flown on wings to get here!"

The Duke laughed because he knew that this was correct.

"Well, I am here now and I hope you have a cool drink waiting for me, because it was hot and dusty on the way down."

"I will order one at once," the equerry replied.

Then he opened the door of Her Majesty's sitting room.

As the Duke was announced and passed into the room, he heard the Queen give a little cry of delight.

He walked towards her and bowed respectfully and, when she held out her hand, he kissed it.

"Do sit down, David, because I have so much to tell you," the Queen began. "I have an important task for you to undertake."

"I am glad to hear that, ma'am. In fact it was what I was hoping I might hear."

"You are not telling me," the Queen said somewhat sardonically, "that you are feeling disenchanted with the gay world that surrounds my son?"

The Duke hesitated for a moment before he replied,

"Not exactly, ma'am, that would be ungracious to those who have been very kind to me. I was just hoping something new would happen, when Your Majesty's letter arrived."

The Queen laughed.

"I knew without you telling me that you would be glad to get away. Although most people in your position, as you well know, would be furious at leaving England in the middle of the Season."

"If that is what I have to do, ma'am, then I can only say that, if it is an unusual and unexpected mission, I will be only too delighted to hear about it."

The Queen settled herself a little more comfortably in the chair she always sat in.

And then she asked the Duke,

"I don't know whether or not you have ever met the brother of Princess Alexandra, who is now King George of Greece?"

"Indeed I have, ma'am, but not recently. And I do know that he was offered the throne when he was only eighteen."

The Queen smiled.

"I thought you would be well informed, David. Of course, as you are aware, George, as he now calls himself, was Prince William of Denmark, but accepted the throne eagerly and has greatly enjoyed being the King of Greece."

Knowing well that Prince William had only been the second son of the King of Denmark and had never expected to rule anywhere, the Duke was not surprised that he enjoyed his position of King.

He also knew that since he had been on the throne there had been a noted expansion of Greece's frontiers, beginning with the cession of the Ionian Islands by Great Britain.

The Duke now wondered how all this concerned him.

He remembered, which had much amused him at the time, that the Prince's father had regarded the Greek throne as a doubtful proposition when it was first offered.

He had therefore not immediately told his son of the offer, but the Prince, however, discovered it himself by reading a newspaper wrapper round a sardine sandwich!

He was delighted at what he read and rushed home and after some difficulty he persuaded his father to let him go to Greece and, despite being so young, his enthusiasm and his intelligence made him, as the years passed by, an excellent King.

Although he was sometimes homesick, he never left Greece during his first four years as King and he threw himself into learning the language and getting to know his people.

The Duke had been sure that because he was so young, it had been a rather lonely road for him. He had to rely a great deal on the advice of Greek politicians, many of whom hoped to exploit him for their own purposes.

But he had turned out to be more astute than they expected.

This all passed through the Duke's mind.

As if the Queen was aware of what he was thinking, she waited for a moment and then said,

"Now I want you to go to Greece and give King George something he will value enormously. But it must be done secretly or I know that there will be trouble with our own people."

The Duke looked at her in surprise, but he did not speak and the Queen continued,

"I know that I can trust you and that you are very clever at subterfuge when you need to be. Otherwise you would not have visited so many strange foreign countries and returned safely to tell the tale."

The Duke chuckled.

"I like to think, ma'am, that my brains have been helpful not only to me but to others I have worked with."

"I know they have, David. That is why I want you to undertake a special secret mission of which no one in England must be aware."

The Duke waited apprehensively.

Then the Queen smiled.

"I know that you never confide in the many women you have courted. Otherwise by this time people would know far more about you than they actually do."

"That is the sort of compliment I really appreciate, ma'am, but quite frankly, the beautiful ladies I know have always wanted me to talk about them rather than about myself!"

"I am sure that is true, David. But most men, and all women, talk too much and this is an occasion when I am very anxious that no one will know what I am doing."

"You can trust me, ma'am," the Duke said quietly.

"I know I can. That is why I am confiding in you."

"I am very honoured, ma'am."

The Queen smiled again.

It flashed through his mind that this was going to be something really new and clearly a challenge.

It was going to be a special mission he had half-anticipated and which he had hoped would occur.

But for the moment he could not possibly think what it could be and he waited impatiently for the Queen to tell him what was in her mind.

As he did so, he could not help feeling a sudden excitement creep over him.

It was what he always felt just before something happened that he had not expected or when he found some treasure he had never thought in his wildest dreams would be his.

It was a feeling that he could not describe in words even to himself.

Yet it was there – the thrill of adventure.

A thrill that he had often thought should be a part of love.

Yet he had never felt it with a woman.

Now as he waited, it was almost as if the sun was moving up the sky and into the room.

He knew even before the Queen spoke that this was what he had been wanting, not only for the last few weeks or months but for much longer than that.

This was the moment when he really felt alive.

It was a thrill that came from his mind and burst through his whole body.

It was a feeling that was indescribable but none the less real.

CHAPTER TWO

The Queen was silent for what seemed a long time and then she said,

"You will understand, I know, that I very much admire the way King George, although so young, has not only reigned in Greece but has captivated all his people."

"You are so right, ma'am. I was talking to a friend of mine recently who had just come back from Greece, and he said it was quite amazing how much the King has done in a comparatively short time. I have been told too by a number of contacts that he has won the affection of all the Greeks."

"George has not only built roads, which apparently did not exist before he arrived, but has tried to restore some of the glory of Greece's past. But there he has a long hard task ahead of him."

The way the Queen spoke told the Duke that this was clearly an important issue and he thought, while she was feeling for the right words, it would be a mistake for him to interrupt.

"You will remember in Ancient Greek history," the Queen went on after a long pause, "that the inhabitants of the Island of Delos, where the God Apollo is believed to have been born, were threatened by the dreaded Persians who arrived at the island with a thousand ships.

"They were on their way to attack Athens and were then defeated at the Battle of Marathon."

The Duke smiled.

"I remember and it must have been a terrible shock to the poor people, although in fact, on the orders of King Darius, they were unharmed."

"It certainly was a shock for them, David, but, if you recall the story, there was much worse to come."

"I think, ma'am, that you are thinking of how four hundred years later the vast Army of King Mithridates of Pontus put to death everyone on the island except those they sold as slaves."

The Queen nodded.

"You certainly know your history, David. I admit to having to revive my memory somewhat on the details."

"The Romans disposed of King Mithridates," the Duke went on, "but alas the damage was done and, though in the fourteenth century the Knights of St. John built a fortress on Delos, they soon abandoned it."

"I read that as well," the Queen said a little sharply and it was as if she rather resented his implying that he knew more than she did.

She paused before she added,

"In time even the name of the island was forgotten. In the seventeenth century the then British Ambassador in Constantinople, Sir Thomas Roe, heard it described as '*a small, despised, uninhabited island, where many rare and interesting artefacts can still be found*'."

"I do remember reading about it, ma'am, and often thought I would go to Delos myself and try to find some of 'the rare artefacts' that have been forgotten."

"That," the Queen smiled, "is what I intend to talk to you about."

The Duke looked surprised as the Queen continued,

"Two hundred years later a treasure was found on Delos which proved the British Ambassador's information to be correct."

"*A treasure*?" the Duke asked in astonishment.

"A very special one indeed and that is what I want to discuss with you."

She lowered her voice, which told the Duke that this was the big secret.

Then he bent forward in his chair so that he should not miss a word.

"Over fifty years ago a British archaeologist, who was an aristocrat, found a very special and very marvellous statue of Apollo on Delos!"

The Duke suppressed an exclamation with some difficulty and the Queen carried on,

"It had lain buried in the ground for a very long time, which presumably had saved it from the vandals and pirates who had destroyed so much on Delos."

"A statue of Apollo!" he repeated almost beneath his breath. "I cannot remember ever seeing one."

The Duke was thinking of the many museums he had visited, especially those in Rome, where there was a profusion of statues stolen from Greece – most of them were of Gods, especially Aphrodite, the Goddess of Love.

Now the Queen went on in a low voice,

"That statue was brought to England and because the finder was frightened that the Greeks, if they heard of it, would demand it back, he hid it here at Windsor Castle."

"Here?" he exclaimed. "How extraordinary!"

"That is what I thought when I first heard about it, David, but it was locked away and I don't think either of my two predecessors had the slightest idea it was here."

The Duke thought that George IV, if no one else, would have appreciated the beauty and significance of it and he would undoubtedly have taken possession of the statue himself.

"I now want, David, to send it back to where it belongs. But you know as well as I do that, if anyone here has the slightest idea of what is happening, they will claim it belongs to England and must remain here."

"I am sure there are a great number of people, ma'am, who would appreciate it," the Duke felt obliged to say.

The Queen smiled.

"And they, of course, would be far more vehement than anyone else in protesting that we must keep it in our possession. They would doubtless then thrust it into a dingy museum."

The Duke was silent, thinking that he agreed with her, but at the same time he could understand the English desire to keep in this country everything they had collected from overseas.

"Now what I intend to do," the Queen asserted, "is to restore to the Greeks the God they still revere and who means far more to them than any of their other Gods or Goddesses."

The Duke knew this to be true.

Apollo, the God of Light and of law and order was, he knew from all he had read and from all he had heard, still in the thoughts of the Greeks.

They paid their respects to Apollo every time they lit a candle in their own homes.

"I feel sure," the Queen said, "that George, as soon as he has the time, will want to restore to Delos some of its former glory."

"From what I have read and heard, ma'am, it has always remained a most holy place in every Greek heart. In Classical days no one was allowed to die there and, if a person was ill, he or she was removed to another island."

"I know and that is why the statue of Apollo, which must be the finest ever carved of him, must go home."

"And so you want me to take it to Delos, ma'am," the Duke enquired simply.

"I trust you, David, and I know that you have the facility of travelling to Greece without anyone being aware that you have a secret mission to accomplish."

The Duke nodded.

"If there is the least suspicion in anyone's mind that I am sending anything so precious out of England, there will be, as you will agree, an outcry from all the collectors and connoisseurs and from our museums both private and public."

The Duke concurred with her wholeheartedly.

"What I want you to do, David, and I know you will do it well, is to take the statue from here at night and if at all possible convey it immediately to the ship you will be travelling in."

"That will be my yacht, ma'am, and you can be assured that it will be perfectly safe there."

"That is what I thought you would say," the Queen replied. "I will write to King George telling him that I feel the restoration of Apollo to his own island will thrill and delight his people. But he must never tell anyone that it came to him from Great Britain."

The Duke nodded his assent to this.

Then the Queen added sharply,

"You must make him realise the trouble there will be for me if anyone has the slightest idea that I have given away anything quite so precious. But I know that you will agree with me that the right place for Apollo is on his own Island of Delos."

"Absolutely, ma'am, but at the same time, because it is unique and so precious, it is undoubtedly a treasure that Britain would love to keep for herself."

"That is what I thought and what I know, but it will, I am sure, help King George more than anything else I could give him."

"I am convinced that you are right, ma'am, and I can only thank you for honouring me with such an unusual and important mission."

"I thought you would find it a change from the life you are leading at the moment, David. And that reminds me, I promised your grandmother that I would speak to you about your future."

The Duke held up his hands.

"No, please, please, ma'am, spare me that! I know only too well and can repeat word for word what my dear grandmother has been saying to you. But my answer is quite simple. I will not marry anyone until I fall in love."

The Queen stared at him.

"Are you telling me that despite your reputation you have never been in love?"

There was silence for a moment and then the Duke replied,

"Not in the way the Greeks thought of love."

"But surely – " the Queen said a little hesitatingly, "you have been in love with some, perhaps one or two, of the lovely ladies who have given their hearts to you?"

The Duke smiled.

"Ma'am, perhaps you will think I am speaking like a Greek when I say that I want the love that Aphrodite told them to find, the love that not only belongs to the heart but to the soul."

For a moment, the Queen gazed at him in surprise.

"You are right, of course, you are so right, David. That is the way I loved Albert – and he loved me."

There was an unmistakable sob in her voice.

Then the Duke added quietly,

"I knew you would understand, ma'am."

"Of course I understand, but somehow I did not expect you to think or feel that way."

"But I do," the Duke answered, "and that is why I have never married."

The Queen looked pensive for a moment.

"Your grandmother begged me to talk to you about marriage. I had, in fact, the idea of asking you to consider a very attractive young Princess whose father, living in Bavaria, needs the support and help of this country."

The Duke knew only too well that the Queen had been endlessly providing Royal brides for bridegrooms in the Balkans for small countries that were being continually threatened by the Russians.

It was, however, a subject he was not particularly interested in and therefore he responded,

"I think, ma'am, before we worry about my affairs, I must go ahead immediately to deliver your most generous and inspiring present to King George."

"I know he will be delighted," the Queen replied. "But it would be dangerous to write to him about it until you actually arrive."

"As soon as I do, ma'am, I will make sure that he realises what a valuable gift he is receiving and how it is essential that the British people never know they have been deprived of such a treasure."

"They will scarcely know what they are missing, since it has been shut up here ever since it reached this country."

"All the same I know that there would be a great to-do if it was known that it had been taken away from them, even though they were not aware of it until that moment."

The Queen laughed.

"I knew you would understand. Although it may be thought of as precious by a few in England, the whole of Greece will be thrilled and delighted if it is restored to where it originally belonged."

"Of course, ma'am, I think you are being very kind and at the same time very wise."

He knew by the expression in her eyes that his praise delighted her.

"What do we do now?" she asked.

"I was just thinking, ma'am, that if you were kind enough to invite me to come back to Windsor and stay for tomorrow night, I could leave soon after midnight when there are no curious eyes about."

He thought for a moment and then continued,

"I will carry the statue with me in a large trunk that I will bring to contain my clothes. Only my valet will be aware it will be that much fuller when I leave than when I arrived!"

The Queen clasped her hands together.

"That is exactly what I hoped you would do. But I must warn you the statue is quite large, almost life-size. Just one of its legs has been slightly damaged."

"I will manage to transport it from here to my yacht which is at present anchored in the Thames. Then, as soon as it is safely aboard, I will leave for Greece."

27

"Leaving many aching hearts and perhaps tearful eyes behind you!"

The Duke laughed.

"I will return," he said, "but Apollo will be back at home and I am sure that all Greece will be on its knees in front of him!"

He knew by the expression on the Queen's face how pleased and excited she was that he had agreed to carry out her mission.

"I will go home now, if ma'am will permit me to do so, and I will mention casually to the equerry who escorts me to my chaise that I will be returning tomorrow night for a party you have invited me to."

"I will arrange the party," the Queen agreed, "but I am sure you will think it would be a great mistake for there to be any Greeks present."

"Of course, ma'am. No one must have the slightest idea where I am going when I leave England. It will take a long time before what will then undoubtedly be a subject of gossip and excitement in Athens gets back to London."

"It is so important that you are never connected in any way with the whole operation," the Queen insisted.

"I will make sure of that," the Duke promised, "and I thank you again, ma'am, for trusting me with such an interesting and exciting adventure."

The Queen smiled.

"Is that how you look upon it, David?"

"It will certainly be something new and different to do and that is what I have been looking for for some time."

Her Majesty held out her hand and the Duke went down on one knee in front of her.

"Your Majesty is very remarkable," he said. "You never cease to surprise those who serve you and those who

28

talk about you. There has never been a woman who has done so much for her country as Your Majesty has done for yours."

"I like to think that is true, David, but alas there are still wars, still people fighting against us."

"That is inevitable, but Britain is greater than she has ever been because Your Majesty is on the throne."

He kissed the Queen's hand.

Then he walked backwards slowly to the door.

The Queen watched him.

Only when the door was then opened by an equerry outside did she exclaim,

"See you tomorrow, my dear Duke, and I am sure you will find it a very amusing party!"

The Duke bowed.

"Your Majesty is always most kind and gracious."

The equerry escorted him down to the front door where his chaise was waiting.

"That was a very short visit, Your Grace," he said. "I hoped you would stay and cheer us up tonight."

"Do you need cheering up?" the Duke enquired.

The equerry wrinkled his nose.

"Shall I say it is not one of our most glamorous house parties at the moment, but, if you were staying, you would cheer us all up!"

"I will be with you tomorrow night," the Duke said, "and I hope Her Majesty will invite some beautiful young ladies to meet me."

The equerry laughed.

"We all wish that, but at present all those staying at Windsor Castle are well past their fiftieth birthday."

The Duke groaned.

"Now you are depressing me. Perhaps I would be wise to have an unexpected call to the country."

"I hope you will not do so," the equerry replied. "Think of us. And I am certain, if you are to be a guest, the Queen will find a few ladies who have not gone grey at their temples!"

The Duke chuckled.

Then he climbed into his chaise.

"Make it your business," he smiled at the equerry, "to see that at least one pretty face sits next to me at dinner or I will have a pressing invitation to visit Paris!"

The equerry laughed and waved as the Duke drove off.

The horses began to gather speed as soon as they were out of the town.

The Duke was thinking that of all the possibilities he had envisaged when on his way to Windsor Castle, such a mission as this had never entered his mind.

Now, when he thought it out, it seemed as if Fate had decreed that he should be blessed.

The task Her Majesty had offered him was unusual and exacting.

There was no doubt that the Queen was correct in thinking that the statue of Apollo should go back to where it belonged.

At the same time if it was known that it had come from England there would be innumerable connoisseurs who would fight fervently to keep it in British hands to the obvious embarrassment of the Queen.

Yet he appreciated that she was indeed wise enough to realise that nothing could be more inspiring for King George at this pivotal moment in his reign.

If he could restore to Delos the God that had been worshipped and adored by every Greek, he too would be a God-like hero.

The Duke remembered reading when at Oxford that it was still believed that a Divine light fell over Delos and to the Greeks Apollo was always present, even as Athena herself was still presiding in the Parthenon.

He recalled thinking that was what he should feel and yet, when he had visited Greece, he found it was a very rough place and he had only stayed for a short time.

It was just before the reign of King George and it was because he had been so interested in the history of Ancient Greece that he had stopped off in Athens.

Yet the Parthenon had moved him in a way he had not expected and he now knew a great deal more about Apollo than he had known then.

The Ancient Greeks had felt that in the air over Delos there was always a dancing quivering flame and it was because Apollo was the God of Light.

The Duke had thought at the time that there was something unmistakably different in the light he had found in Greece.

Then he had read that some people who paid a visit to Delos were aware, in the bright shimmering light, of the beating of silver wings and a whir of silver wheels.

It was, he believed, just a romantic fantasy of those who wrote about the Greek Islands.

Now it occurred to the Duke that perhaps because he was to be the conveyor of Apollo, he too should know all about this.

Then he told himself he was just being ridiculous and because he was English and practical, he could hardly feel what the Ancient Greeks had felt.

Or, as they had fervently believed, that the Gods watched over them and directed every single thought and movement of their lives.

'I am letting my imagination run away with me,' he mused as he neared London.

Then he remembered that he was dining with the Prince of Wales tonight.

It would be a huge mistake to say he had been at Windsor Castle during the day, even more of a mistake for the Prince to think that in any way his mother had confided in him.

Queen Victoria had always prevented her son from taking any part in State affairs and this drove him, as the Duke and others of his friends and admirers knew, into a life that was a waste of his brain and intelligence.

So, because he had nothing else to do, the Prince pursued women, falling in and out of love as easily as the Duke himself.

Yet, whenever they appeared together in public, the Prince and his wife, Princess Alexandra, seemed an ideal married couple and it was therefore not surprising that the people applauded them.

Only the close friends of the Prince, like the Duke, knew how much he yearned to be involved in State affairs and how much he longed to be allowed to be present at the private meetings when the Queen learnt the truth of all that was occurring in every part of her Empire.

But the door was shut against him and he returned to his pursuit of women simply because he was barred so unreasonably from taking his rightful place as heir to the throne of Great Britain.

'I must be very careful,' the Duke told himself as they neared Park Lane, 'that His Royal Highness does not connect, in any way, my departure from London the day after tomorrow with the fact that I have visited Windsor Castle twice this week.'

He knew that the Prince of Wales was extremely curious and desperate to learn what his mother confided to his friends, while he himself was shut out completely.

*

The Duke drew up outside Sherbourne House.

As he did so, he noticed there was a closed carriage outside the front door.

And he did not have to look twice at the footman's livery to know who was calling on him.

She might well be beautiful, which she undoubtedly was, but at the same time, she was a talker.

She always knew the tit-bits of news that amused and sometimes shocked those in the *Beau Monde*.

As the Duke handed his hat and gloves to one of his footman, the butler intoned,

"Lady Evelyn is here waiting for Your Grace in the drawing room."

The Duke glanced at the clock on the mantelpiece.

Then the butler added,

"I've ordered the closed carriage for Your Grace at seven o'clock."

'That,' the Duke thought, 'will give me very little time with Lady Evelyn.'

He knew she had called on him because she had expected him to visit her during the afternoon or at least to send her a message if he could not come.

He had meant to visit her, but being summoned to Windsor Castle had made it impossible and he was now wondering what his excuse could be as the butler opened the door of the drawing room.

He had just started his affair with Lady Evelyn.

She had a husband who disliked London and spent most of his time in the country, while she held court at one of the most impressive houses in Regent's Park.

As she was exceedingly wealthy in her own right, her husband could not accuse her of extravagance, but the whole of London chattered about the magnificence of her dinner parties where everyone ate off gold plates.

She gave balls, where the garden was lit by fairy lights and she hired the best musicians, actors and actresses to entertain her friends when the conversation ran out.

The Duke had not paid any particular attention to Lady Evelyn until they had met at Marlborough House.

She had then insisted, saying she was nervous of being driven at night without an escort, that he should see her home.

That was when she had made it very clear that, if he was interested, so was she, as his own carriage followed behind.

The Duke was quite certain that with two stalwart servants of her own she was perfectly safe, although there was some justification for her feeling nervous.

The amount of jewellery she wore would certainly be a great temptation to any robber. They were not only heirlooms from her husband's family, but also they were from her own collection of diamonds, emeralds and rubies.

Her jewels were the envy of every woman in the *Beau Monde* and they sparkled round her long white neck and in her dark hair.

Her gowns made every woman anywhere near her look dowdy and somehow out of date.

She was waiting for him, reclining on a sofa.

The first thing the Duke saw as he entered the room were the ostrich feathers on her bonnet and they swayed a little as she turned her head towards him.

She was very beautiful, there was no denying that.

Yet for a moment, because his mind was on Greece and Apollo, the Duke unexpectedly found her not at all alluring.

She was certainly not as intriguing as all that lay ahead of him.

"David!" she exclaimed as he moved towards her. "How could you leave London without telling me where you were going?"

"You must forgive me," the Duke murmured as he reached her.

He took her ungloved hand in his and raised it to his lips, but he did not quite touch her skin.

"You look very beautiful today," he remarked, "and I am very sorry that I could not call on you, as I intended to do after luncheon."

"Where have you been?" she asked imperiously. "And how could anything be more important than that we should be together?"

"I think I should ask that question of you first," the Duke said. "You must tell me where *you* have been, what you have done and who has told you in my absence that you are surely the most beautiful woman in London."

Lady Evelyn laughed a little and looked up at him with an expression on her face he knew only too well.

"Did you really miss me?" she asked. "Were you a little jealous that someone might have taken your place?"

"Of course I was jealous, Evelyn, and I will tell you about it tomorrow. But now, as I am sure you are aware, I am dining with His Royal Highness tonight, and to be late is an unforgivable sin. I must now go and dress."

"How can you possibly be so unkind as to dine at Marlborough House when you could dine with me?" Lady Evelyn pouted.

"Unfortunately His Royal Highness invited me a week ago. I was not aware at that time that I could be with you."

"But I want you now, this moment, and I want you to dine with *me* tonight. We will be all alone as I have deliberately not asked anyone else."

There was no doubt, from the way she spoke and the way she looked at him, what she intended.

But the Duke could not help feeling that this was a line he had heard before.

"You must forgive me, Evelyn, and tomorrow I will go on my knees to make sure you do. But now unless I am to be sent to the Tower of London for lese-majesty I have to go and dress."

Before she could reply, he kissed both her hands.

Then, even as her fingers tried to tighten on his, he had crossed the room and was standing at the door.

"You are not to tempt me, Evelyn, and the only way I can be safe from such temptation is to leave you. Goodnight, my beautiful one, and when you sleep, dream of me."

He was gone before she could bat an eyelid.

He ruminated, as he ran up the stairs, towards his bedroom that she would undoubtedly never forgive him, especially when he did not turn up tomorrow night either.

His bath was waiting for him and Jenkins had laid out his clothes.

Because he had been a soldier, he was always quick in everything he did.

He had bathed, dressed and was hurrying down the stairs in record time.

'Two records in one day!' he told himself as he stepped into his carriage.

Because the coachman knew that he must not be late, the horses were actually moving before the door of the carriage was closed by the footman.

As he leant back comfortably, he was not thinking of the lovely Lady Evelyn, who had gone away angry and tight-lipped.

His thoughts were all of tomorrow night at Windsor Castle, when he would take away the statue of the God Apollo from its English hiding place and restore him in glory to his own country, and there his own people would revere him, as they had done more than two thousand years ago.

The Duke was still thinking of Apollo as he drove swiftly towards Marlborough House.

Some words he thought he had long forgotten, but which he had read at Oxford, came to his mind,

"Apollo ruled the world by the power of his beauty. He had no earthly resources, no Army, no Navy and no powerful Government. In the beginning his sole possession was a barren Island."

But, as the Duke told himself, he became the most worshipped of all the Greek Gods and he typified to his people the beauty of Light and of Reason.

And that was why he must now return to the land that needed not only his light but his heart.

CHAPTER THREE

Dinner at Marlborough House was as usual most amusing.

There were a number of extremely pretty ladies and gentlemen with whom the Duke enjoyed conversing.

When the ladies left the dining room, the gentlemen talked politics.

As they were finishing a decanter of port, one of them remarked,

"You should attend The House of Lords more often, David. Your ideas might be a little revolutionary, but you have convinced me that they are valid."

The Duke smiled.

"I am afraid I find the speeches boring, especially when the older members read them rather badly."

There was some laughter at his comment and then someone sneered,

"The only things you read, Sherbourne, are *billets doux*."

"That is an insult," the Duke fumed. "I ought to call you out tomorrow morning."

"That would certainly be very unfair," the Prince of Wales intervened. "David is a very good shot and I bet no one is quicker than he is."

"The trouble with David," someone chipped in, "is that he is so quick at everything, especially where a pretty woman is concerned!"

They were all laughing at the Duke again, but he enjoyed it.

All the same they all assumed he was not interested in anything but enjoying himself.

They would indeed be surprised if they knew what he was planning to do tomorrow.

After dinner some of the gentlemen played bridge and the ladies flirted with those who were not sitting at the bridge tables.

It was after twelve o'clock when the party finally broke up.

When the Duke said goodnight to his host, His Royal Highness said,

"Come and dine with me again soon, David. You always make the party go and you certainly scored points off his Lordship."

"I always enjoy myself at Marlborough House," the Duke replied. "Thank you, sir, so very much for the most delicious dinner and an enjoyable time."

The Prince of Wales was obviously pleased at the compliment and patted him on the shoulder.

"You will be receiving an invitation from me in the next day or two," he added.

The Duke thought it wise not to answer this, so he merely hurried to where his carriage was waiting to drive him home.

Late though it was, he was wondering how he could pack the statue of Apollo safely and securely.

It had been quite a shock when Her Majesty had told him the statue was almost life-size, as he had been thinking of it as a sculpture that would stand on an altar or in some special alcove in a Chapel.

He had said lightly that it would fit easily into his luggage, but he certainly did not have a trunk large enough for a statue that was almost life-size.

When he arrived back at his house, instead of going to his bedroom, he went up to the attics where he knew his luggage and old suitcases were stored.

He carried with him a lighted candle and then he lit another so that he could inspect the enormous number of pieces of luggage that had accumulated in the attics over the years.

His own cases were smart and of the best leather, but when he looked at them they were all far too small for anything like this statue.

He knew that it would be a great mistake for it to be simply wrapped up in linen as that would obviously make the servants at Windsor Castle question what he was taking away and for them to talk about it would be dangerous.

'There must be something,' he said to himself as he looked around.

Then, at the far end of the attic, he saw what looked for a moment almost like a bed placed against the wall.

For a while, he stared at it and then he remembered what it was.

When he had been on a trip to Japan, he had seen two delightfully embroidered and bejewelled screens that had been made perhaps a hundred years ago.

They were in their own way unique and he had brought them home and one of them was in his castle in the country. The other, because it was rather large, was in a room he seldom used in London.

They had, in fact, turned out to be white elephants as they did not fit in with any of the rest of his furniture or decorative schemes.

To bring them home he had had a special packing case designed to hold them and this was now staring at him across the attic.

As he looked at it, he knew exactly what he would do.

He went back downstairs and found his valet, as he had expected, in his bedroom.

Jenkins had realised his Master had gone upstairs and thought it very strange that he should be visiting the attics so late at night.

As he came into his bedroom, the Duke called out to Jenkins,

"I have promised Her Majesty that I would give her a present. It has to be something rather good as actually I forgot her birthday this year."

"I thinks you were abroad, Your Grace."

"I intend to make up for it now," the Duke went on, as if Jenkins had not spoken, "by giving her one of the screens you will remember we brought back with us from Japan."

"Her Majesty will like that, I'm sure, but if you remember, Your Grace, they were a terrible nuisance to us on the voyage, being too big to be put into the cabins, and people complained they tripped over them when they stood in the corridor."

"I remember, Jenkins, but we brought them home safely. I want you first thing tomorrow morning to bring down the case that was made for them in Japan and put the screen which is in the blue drawing room into it."

"I'll have to have some help, Your Grace."

"Yes, of course. Get the footmen to help you, but be certain you supervise it properly so that the screen is not damaged in any way before I present it to Her Majesty."

"When'll Your Grace be doing that?"

"Some time tomorrow, Jenkins, and I will let you know exactly when. But have the screen packed up first thing in the morning."

He gave the order almost sharply so that he knew it would be carried out.

He had no intention of telling Jenkins until much later that they were going away as he did not want there to be too much speculation as to 'whys and wherefores' in the servants' hall.

When the Duke at last climbed into bed, it was with a feeling of satisfaction that he had settled one problem.

The large case for the screens would definitely hold a life-size statue.

*

The Duke slept peacefully and so did not think of Lady Evelyn until the following day.

He rode his best stallion at seven o'clock in Rotten Row as he always did.

He saw a number of friends and received several invitations to which he avoided a direct answer.

Then, when he returned to his house, he sent for his secretary.

He told him he was to refuse every invitation he received for the next two weeks.

Mr. Simmonds was astonished.

"But Your Grace has already accepted so many engagements," he protested.

"I am aware of that, Simmonds, so I want you to tell everyone that I have been called away unexpectedly to Scotland as one of my relatives is very ill and the doctors don't think he will live very long."

Mr. Simmonds had been with the Duke ever since he came into the title and he knew only too well that, once the Duke had made up his mind, it was no use arguing with him.

However, he gave a deep sigh, knowing he would have to cope with a lot of indignant people, especially the ladies who would be hurt and upset at losing him.

"I want you to send, late this afternoon," the Duke went on, "a large bouquet of orchids to Lady Evelyn. I will give you a letter to go with it."

Mr. Simmonds sighed again.

He knew how voluble Lady Evelyn would be if the Duke disappeared to Scotland, but there was no point in saying so.

The Duke gave Mr. Simmonds other instructions, the most important of which was that he was to say nothing to the household, not even to his valet, until later in the afternoon.

He knew he could trust Mr. Simmonds implicitly and that he would obey all his instructions to the letter.

Equally he was well aware that the Duke had no dying relative in Scotland and so he was wondering where the Duke was going and who was going with him.

"Last, but not least," the Duke added, "I am dining tonight at Windsor Castle, but it is most important that no one in London is aware of it."

Mr. Simmonds looked at him in surprise.

"Send a message now to Captain Holt that I will be coming aboard *The Mermaid* some time after midnight, and, as soon as I am aboard, I wish the yacht to sail down the Thames immediately."

"Then you are actually going to Scotland, Your Grace," Mr. Simmonds commented, a little bewildered.

"It may be Scotland or it may be elsewhere," the Duke told him. "But I want to just slip away without there being any fuss or talk about it. So I trust you not to say a word of what is happening until I have actually left for Windsor Castle."

He knew that Mr. Simmonds was confused, also a little hurt that he was not being trusted completely with the arrangements.

But the Duke thought it wiser to say nothing more.

He had a luncheon engagement at his Club with a gentleman who wished to ask his advice on some personal matters to include his horses.

The Duke enjoyed the conversation and he did not return to the house until three o'clock.

It was then, as he went through the front door, he saw the packing case that he knew contained the screen.

It was neatly fastened and, he thought, since it had contained two screens originally, that it was definitely big enough for the statue.

He wrote his letters and sent for Mr. Simmonds.

"There is no hurry for the letter that goes with the flowers," he said. "Lady Evelyn will not be expecting me until at least eight o'clock and I should like this letter and the flowers to arrive not more than an hour earlier."

It was, he admitted to himself, rather unkind to let her down at the last moment when she was expecting him for an evening of love.

But he had to prevent her from finding out that, if he was going to travel to Scotland, he was dining first at Windsor Castle.

It might be discovered later, but then he would be on the high seas and there would be nothing anyone could do about it.

The Duke wrote several other letters of apology for having to cancel an engagement, but he did not think that any of the recipients would be particularly curious about which of his relatives was ill.

It was four o'clock when he sent for Jenkins.

"I need your assistance, your help and your silence, Jenkins."

He liked the alert look that came into the man's eyes.

Jenkins had been with the Duke ever since he had entered the Army, when he had been his batman and, when he surrendered his Commission, Jenkins left with him.

He had travelled with him in all the years when he was exploring what he could of the world and, as the Duke knew better than anyone else, Jenkins was invaluable.

He enjoyed everything even if it was uncomfortable or dangerous and he never lost his temper nor his sense of humour.

The Duke had found him an admirable companion in the most difficult and unusual situations.

As Jenkins waited to receive his orders, the Duke said with a smile,

"This is secret, Jenkins, and so no one must know where we are going or why."

Jenkins's eyes twinkled.

"I were just thinking, Your Grace, that things be a bit dull lately."

"Pack everything I require for quite a long journey and be as quick as possible."

"Will it be hot or cold, Your Grace?"

"Fairly hot and evening clothes as well as day."

What he liked about Jenkins was that he asked no more questions, merely enquiring,

"What time will us be leaving, Your Grace?"

"At half-past five," the Duke replied, "because I are dining at Windsor Castle before we go any further."

Jenkins merely nodded and still asked no questions and the Duke knew his clothes would be ready together with his revolver in one of the cases.

Jenkins was as excited at going abroad as he was.

They finally started off, travelling not in the smart light chaise but in a much larger one in which there was room for plenty of luggage.

As they drove out of London, the Duke knew that Jenkins was looking forward to all that lay ahead.

They could not travel to Windsor Castle as fast as the Duke had the day before.

Then there had been nothing on board the chaise except himself and a groom. Now there was a large amount of luggage as well as the screen.

Although he could have sent the luggage directly to his yacht in the Thames, the Duke knew that would tell the servants that he was going away.

It would then only be a question of a short time before the whole of London would be avidly buzzing with speculation.

Servants talked to servants and the Duke had learnt very early in life that the fewer the people who knew what you were doing, the safer it was.

They arrived at Windsor Castle exactly at the time he had intended, which was just before seven-thirty.

He wanted to give Her Majesty her present before dinner.

If the other dinner guests were to see it, the less interest they would take if they saw the case leaving on his carriage later that night.

An equerry greeted the Duke and he asked if his present for the Queen could be taken to her private sitting room.

The equerry looked at him in astonishment.

"I really cannot imagine what you are giving Her Majesty," he queried, "but it's certainly *very large*."

"You will surely admire it when you see it," the Duke replied. "I want the case to be opened as soon as I have presented it to her."

Jenkins was then taken away by a servant with the luggage the Duke would require that evening.

The rest of the trunks on the Duke's instructions remained in the carriage and he gave orders that it was not to be unloaded when the horses were put into the stables.

Anyone who served the Duke knew only too well that it was a disastrous mistake not to obey his orders to the letter however strange they might seem.

As the Duke walked up the stairs to Her Majesty's private apartments, he was sure everything would now go smoothly.

The Queen had already received some of her guests when the large case containing the screen was carried into her sitting room.

"What can that be, David?" she enquired sharply.

The Duke, who was just behind, piped up at once,

"A present that I hope will please you, Your Majesty."

She met his eyes and understood that this was all part of the game.

"How exciting," she then cooed in a different tone of voice. "I cannot imagine what it is."

"I want it to be opened in front of Your Majesty," the Duke said, "so I hope to be forgiven if it makes rather a mess."

"Now you are making me really curious, David."

The Duke recognised that she was astute enough to understand why the packing case was so necessary.

While the servants began to untie it, making quite a commotion as they went about it, she watched without any comment.

When finally the screen was taken out, she gave an exclamation of delight.

"How lovely and just how beautiful!" she enthused. "Where could you have found such an unusual piece?"

"It came from Japan, ma'am. It is over a hundred years old and I thought that Your Majesty would appreciate it. It will also keep the draughts from your back."

The Queen laughed and replied,

"It is lovely and thank you very very much. It is something I will always cherish."

The Duke had already instructed Jenkins that all the packing was to be taken to his room together with the case.

He was to tell the staff confidentially that it was important for him to keep it because he had actually bought two screens at the same time.

The servants cleared it all away while the Queen was appreciating the fine workmanship of the screen and ordering it to be placed behind the chair she always sat in.

"It's a perfect background for Your Majesty," one of her guests commented.

"It is so clever of the Duke," the Queen replied, "to know that this is exactly what I need in this room, but I could not find anything quite so pretty or so colourful in England."

"None of us could embroider as well as this," one lady remarked.

Another lady was inspecting the workmanship and saying it was something she was determined to copy in one way or another.

At the very least, the Duke reflected, it had taken the interest away from him.

He was certain that tomorrow they would still be talking about the screen rather than speculating as to why he had left Windsor Castle so early.

Dinner was as usual quite homely food without any pretensions about it and one might have said the same about the wine.

When dinner was over and some of the guests then settled down to play bridge, the Queen was able to have a whispered word with the Duke.

"Here is the key to the room in which the statue has been ever since it came to Windsor Castle," she said. "You will need to take a light with you. It is standing on the left hand side of the room not far from the door, and it is wrapped up in a red blanket so you cannot confuse it with anything else."

"That makes it very much easier, ma'am," the Duke murmured.

"I inspected the room myself this morning," the Queen added, "making an excuse that I was afraid the roof might be leaking in that room as it was in another room nearby."

The Duke was listening intently.

"I therefore was able to have the statue moved nearer the door from where it had been put years ago. In case the ceiling leaked on that and several other valuable antiques, I had them covered with blankets. I actually put a red one over Apollo myself. I know no one will dare to touch it."

"Your Majesty is very sensible. I will leave soon after everyone retires with the excuse that I have received bad news about a relative. I will tell those who assist us downstairs that my valet had picked up the letters when we were leaving London and I had no time to open them until now."

He paused before he added,

"I will ask the Officer in Charge to explain to Your Majesty that bad news from a close relative who is dying in Scotland had forced me to leave so unexpectedly."

"You do think of everything, David, and I am most grateful to you, as well as telling you once again you are very resourceful."

"I only hope Your Majesty will always think so."

It was then impossible to say any more.

Only when all the guests had said goodnight did the Queen, when he bowed over her hand, whisper,

"Good luck, David!"

The Duke went to his bedroom and was reassured that Jenkins had everything packed and ready.

Without speaking, he followed the Duke down the corridor to a part of Windsor Castle that was not often used and was therefore in darkness.

With a light from the candles they both carried, it was not difficult for the Duke to find the right room. The Queen had explained exactly where it was.

He turned the key in the lock.

When they went into the room, the first thing the Duke noticed was the red blanket just a little to his left.

He had already told Jenkins what they were looking for.

The Duke found that the statue, which came up to his shoulder, was wrapped with the red blanket and a white linen material round the whole body.

The difficulty was that, when the two men lifted the statue up between them, it was too heavy for them to carry anything else and it was impossible to manage the candles at the same time.

It was the Duke who solved the problem by first carrying Apollo out of the room where he had stood for so many years and locking the door behind them.

Then he sent Jenkins to place a candle as far down the passage as they could see.

When he came back, they carried the statue to the candle.

Repeating this procedure made the journey back to the Duke's room a long and difficult one and fortunately they managed it without anyone being aware that they were moving about.

And it was with a feeling of some relief when they reached the Duke's bedroom.

Neither had spoken since the Duke had suggested what they should do with the candles and, only as the door closed, did Jenkins say,

"Whatever that there piece of stone weighs, I hopes I don't have to carry it much further!"

"I hope not either," the Duke replied. "But first we must pack it up so that no one will see what we are taking away with us."

The large packing case in which they had brought the screen fortunately fitted Apollo exactly.

In case he should roll about in it, the Duke wrapped him in another blanket as well as in the packing they had used for the screen.

It was, as he had anticipated, nearly one o'clock when finally Jenkins collected the night servants to carry the Duke's personal luggage, including Apollo, down to his carriage.

The Officer in Charge of the security that night was told the same story the Duke had invented earlier – that owing to his haste in leaving London, he had brought his letters with him and had only just read them.

One of them had told him that a close relative was on the point of dying in Scotland and he only hoped he could reach him in time.

The Officer in Charge understood his predicament and promised that he would explain to Her Majesty in the morning why he had been obliged to leave immediately for London.

"I know Her Majesty will appreciate my urgency," the Duke said. "Of course, if I had not been so busy all day, I would have read my letters earlier and would not have waited until after dinner. But, as you will understand, I was afraid of being late."

"I do see, Your Grace," the Officer replied. "It is what we all worry about, especially as Her Majesty herself is always so punctual."

"I can only apologise for causing such a commotion in the middle of the night and being such a trouble to you."

"You have been no trouble at all," the Officer said politely. "I only hope that Your Grace will be in time."

"I will certainly try to be," the Duke sighed.

He tipped all the servants who had conveyed his luggage downstairs and helped place it in his carriage.

He realised, although he did not say so, that they were surprised at the size and weight of the largest case.

*

Then at last the Duke had the reins in his hands and they were driving out of the courtyard and onto the road.

He thought that by the mercy of God and with the undoubted help of his Guardian Angel, he had managed to depart without anyone showing any curiosity or being in the least suspicious of what he had taken away with him.

He was sure no one could realise that the packing case, which had been quite heavy when they arrived, was *very* much heavier when they left. Luckily it had been carried out by servants who had just come on duty.

It was only when they were driving back to London as quickly as they could, and the Duke was grateful there was a moon to show the way, that Jenkins asked,

"Your Grace has not told me where we be going."

"That is to be a surprise until we are at sea. I want no speculation amongst the crew, so we will merely say we are making for the Mediterranean."

"That suits me," Jenkins replied. "I only hopes I've packed the right clothes for Your Grace, if we are being entertained by the Frenchies or them Arabs on the other side of it!"

The Duke laughed.

"I will leave you guessing as to which side of the Mediterranean we are visiting until we are nearer. But, as I have told you already, Jenkins, this is a secret mission and the less interest anyone shows in it the better."

"You can trust me, Your Grace, as you've done so often before, to keep me mouth shut."

The Duke knew this was true.

Jenkins had always been a magnificent servant on all their travels and he had never once betrayed to anyone anything his Master had told him confidentially.

"Well, one thing's for sure," Jenkins remarked as the Duke did not speak. "We be getting something new, and that's always what Your Grace wants and I wants too!"

"You are quite right, Jenkins. If nothing else, this voyage will bring us new ideas and new interests."

They drove on in silence.

Only when they neared the Thames did Jenkins say excitedly,

"There be *The Mermaid*! I can see her sure enough through them trees."

The Duke knew that the Captain of *The Mermaid* would tie up as near as he could to the House of Lords, which had always been a favourite place for those who were rich enough to possess yachts.

As he drew up on the Embankment, three of his seamen, who were obviously on the lookout for him, ran towards the carriage.

Glancing up at Big Ben, the Duke saw that it was just after two o'clock in the morning.

Having handed over his horses to the groom, he now walked aboard, leaving Jenkins to instruct the seamen to carry the luggage to his cabin.

Next to the Master cabin there was a smaller one that was usually used by the most important guest.

It was the most comfortable and quite the prettiest of all the other cabins in the yacht.

Jenkins had the large case containing Apollo put in there. Then he locked the door and handed the Duke the key.

"Although Your Grace's said nothing about it," he said, "I thinks that everyone that sees that big packing case is going to be curious as to what's inside it. If you asks me, I think it should be under lock and key."

"You are quite right and I should have thought of that myself. But as you know, Jenkins, I can always rely on you."

Jenkins did not reply and then quickly unpacked the Duke's nightclothes and laid them ready for him in the Master cabin.

Then, as the Duke had ordered in his letter to the Captain, they cast off and the yacht moved out into the middle of the Thames.

By the time the Duke was undressed and in the very comfortable bed that he had chosen himself when he was building the yacht, *The Mermaid* was already some way down the river.

The Duke thought as he lay down that everything had gone as if on greased wheels. He could hardly believe himself that it had all seemed so simple.

His letter to the Queen purported to explain how sorry and disappointed he was to have to rush away to the deathbed of one of his relatives and he said at the end that he would keep Her Majesty well informed of anything that happened during his journey.

He felt sure that she would also like to know the condition of his relative when he arrived at his destination and he thought to himself it was a letter that told the Queen everything she would need to know.

There would be no hint of its inner meaning if anyone else read it and no one would find anything strange or particularly interesting in it.

He was confident that no one at Windsor Castle would have any idea that he had taken out more than he had brought in.

When they heard the reason for his leaving, none of the house party would be particularly curious as to why his departure had been at night.

'At least I have set off on the right foot,' the Duke mused to himself.

Then, because it had actually been a long and tiring day, he quickly fell asleep.

*

When he awoke, they were already out to sea and small waves were breaking over the bow of *The Mermaid.*

As he sat up in bed, he realised that he had done it and he could congratulate himself on a very neat and smart piece of work.

He was sure that no one at Windsor Castle would guess that anything was missing from the large collection of different objects in the room from which he had taken the statue of Apollo.

No one on board would give a thought to the extra luggage he had brought with him even if it did seem heavy.

The only difficulty now was to convey the statue of Apollo to the King of Greece without anyone realising it came from England.

He had not yet thought this problem out clearly.

But he was sure that having gone so far he must not now fail in delivering the precious goods without anyone knowing where the statue had come from.

'I must think of something,' the Duke reflected. 'It will certainly give me a puzzle to occupy my mind until we reach Athens.'

Equally he felt excited at what lay ahead.

He told himself that so far he had succeeded in one of the most difficult tasks that had ever been set for him.

In the past he had taken many of his friends on *The Mermaid* and he had also been accompanied occasionally by some particularly attractive young woman.

But he had found, as many men before him had found, that few women were at their best at sea and most of them were seasick if it was at all rough.

The Duke therefore had either travelled alone on *The Mermaid* or had been joined by a man as interested as he was in visiting new places and new countries.

There was now one last fence to surmount.

It was he and he alone who must now convey to the King of Greece the present that the Queen had sent him, without anyone else being aware of where the statue came from.

It was not going to be easy, of that he was quite certain.

He hoped he would find an answer to the problem before they reached Athens or at least soon after his arrival.

He was quite sure that there was not a single person in the whole of England, except the Queen, who knew that the statue had left Windsor Castle and was actually lying in the cabin next to his.

What he had to do now was to give it back to the country from which it had come without anyone realising that their most beloved God had been brought home.

It was just the sort of problem the Duke enjoyed solving.

He thought with a little thrill of excitement that, as the first fences had been taken without any disaster, he had to take the last fence as if was a triumph.

'I have to think of a way,' he told himself.

However, just for the moment he could only think with satisfaction that he was at sea and no one was the slightest bit interested in what lay locked in the cabin next to his.

CHAPTER FOUR

The Duke woke with a feeling of satisfaction.

Although he would not admit it, he was thrilled to be aboard his yacht again.

The Bay of Biscay was fairly rough, but not as bad as it had been on other occasions.

He spent a great deal of time on the bridge with the Captain, as he found that when he was there he forgot the problems that lay ahead.

But, when he went to bed in his comfortable Master cabin, he wondered again how he could possibly give the statue of Apollo to the Greek King without anyone being aware that it came from England.

He turned the problem over and over in his mind and felt there must be a solution if only he could find it.

The Mediterranean was calm, blue and warm.

It was a joy to feel *The Mermaid* rushing through the water and not to have to think, for the moment, of anything but enjoying himself.

Yet inevitably the conundrum was back again in his mind.

He knew that whatever else he did he must not let the Queen down.

They arrived at Piraeus, the port of Athens, rather sooner than he had expected, which pleased the Duke and he congratulated the crew.

He left Jenkins in charge of the locked cabin and went ashore, finding a suitable carriage to take him the five miles to the Palace in Athens.

He had been rather afraid that the King and his family would be at Tatoi, their heavily wooded estate in the country.

He had heard from visitors that the King felt this was their home rather than the immense German-Grecian Palace that King Otho had built in Athens.

However, the driver of the carriage that conveyed him through new streets, which had not been there on his previous visit, told him that the King and Queen were in Athens.

The Duke wondered if, in fact, he would find a large party at the Palace, but he knew from what he had heard that King George kept the formality of his Court to a minimum, insisting on as little pomp and ceremony as possible.

The Duke had met Queen Olga on his previous visit and was looking forward to meeting her again.

He knew the romantic story of the way she had met the King and how they had fallen in love with each other.

The first visit of King George to the Court of Czar Alexander II was in 1861, the year before he became King of Greece and it was there he first met the Grand Duchess Olga, who was only twelve years old at the time.

Olga was the only daughter of the Czar's brother Constantine, and her mother was Princess Alexandra of Sachsen-Altenburg.

She was very bright and intelligent, spending her time between the Imperial Court and her father's estate and as she grew older, she developed into the prettiest and most charming Princess.

It was not until the spring of 1867 that King George left to pay a State Visit to Russia accompanied by a large retinue.

There he met the young Grand Duchess Olga again, now grown up.

He fell in love with her straightaway and she with him and by the time he left to return to Greece the marriage was fixed for the following October.

The ceremony took place according to the rites both of the Orthodox and the Lutheran Churches and the Czar celebrated it with great pageantry and circumstance.

The Winter Palace and the whole Capital blazed with illuminations and endless festivities.

At the conclusion of the Thanksgiving Services, balls, State dances and other Court functions, the newly married bride and bridegroom retired to Tsarskoye-Selo.

A little later they set out for the new Queen's future home and then the Greek people received their young and beautiful Queen with wild enthusiasm.

The Duke thought Queen Olga's great popularity was due not only to her charming simplicity, but to her sympathy and understanding, which had not been present in the previous reign.

The Duke had been told repeatedly that the Queen gave sympathetic assistance wherever it was needed and ever since she had set foot on Greek soil, she continually made the people aware that she was always there to listen to them if they were in trouble.

What was more and what had astonished the other nations round them, was that she had been untiring in her endeavours to raise the position of women in Society.

All these thoughts passed through the Duke's mind.

While he was impressed, as he always had been by her, he was really wondering how the Queen could help him in his present difficulties.

As the Duke drove up the hill to the Palace and saw it ahead of him, he realised, as he had the first time he visited Greece, that it had been built on a very large scale.

It was more than capable of accommodating two or three Royal Families, but the German architect had not been a very practical man.

Two large inner courtyards took up nearly half the total area and the Duke remembered the system of passages and corridors that were as broad as some of the new streets in Athens.

Looking back, he well remembered that, besides the Banqueting Hall on the ground floor, the Royal Family had a large dining room on the first floor.

He hoped that he might be asked to share a meal with them, but it depended on how long he was to remain in Athens.

It would be a great mistake, as Queen Victoria had pointed out to him, for him to be welcomed too publicly by the Greek King.

One thing he remembered on his last visit was that, although the King and Queen talked Danish to each other, the conversation was usually in English.

The carriage came to a stop outside the impressive entrance and, as the Duke then climbed out, servants in distinctive uniforms threw open the door.

When he informed them that he wished to see the King and gave his name, he was taken along the corridors that seemed almost more elaborate and complicated than they had on his first visit.

There were several equerries on duty outside what was obviously the King's private sitting room.

In a surprisingly short time, the Duke was ushered in.

It was several years since he had seen King George.

Now he had grown somewhat in stature and as the Duke remembered when he faced him, they were not only the same age but almost identical in height.

"What a surprise to see you, David!" King George exclaimed. "But I am so delighted you are here and I hope you will be staying for a long visit."

"I hope so too, sir," the Duke replied. "And I have brought a number of messages for you from your friends in England that I know you will want to hear."

As he spoke, he glanced over his shoulder to make quite sure that the door into the passage was closed and he had not been followed into the room by an equerry.

As if he sensed their conversation was to be private, the King walked to the fireplace, which it being summer was filled with flowers, at the other end of the room.

He sat down on a sofa.

"If you join me here, David," he said, "nothing we say to each other can be overheard."

The Duke smiled.

"So you realise, sir, that our conversation is to be secret."

"I had the impression that you had something to tell me as soon as you entered the room, and I am right, am I not?"

"You certainly are, sir!"

Then, lowering his voice so that it was barely above a whisper, he told the King exactly why he was there.

King George's eyes widened.

The Duke realised that it had never entered his head for one moment that he should receive such a present from Queen Victoria.

Only when the Duke had finished his story, did he exclaim,

"I cannot believe it! How could Her Majesty be so kind and so understanding?"

"She was thinking of Your Majesty with admiration and feeling sure it was something that would help you."

"Help me! It is what I have been longing for and praying for. We have excavated a large amount of the Island of Delos, but while we did find bits and pieces of statues that had been smashed by pirates and the Turks, there was no a sign of Apollo himself."

"I have not actually seen the statue I have brought with me," the Duke told him, "but I do believe it is almost intact and I am sure it is one of the most important statues of the God ever sculpted."

"I really don't know how to thank Her Majesty for her kindness," the King sighed.

"There is one great problem," added the Duke.

"What can that be?" the King asked.

"No one, either here in Greece or in England, must know where the statue has come from or that Her Majesty Queen Victoria has had anything to do with your receiving it."

The King nodded.

"I can understand. The British would be extremely annoyed to find that anything so precious had been taken away from them."

"Of course," the Duke agreed. "Therefore, sir, we have to think of how I can give you what is hidden in my yacht without some curious eyes spying on us."

"Now I see your problem, David, but we have to think of a foolproof solution."

There was silence for a moment and then the Duke suggested,

"I was thinking last night that perhaps the best idea would be for me to deposit it secretly on Delos."

King George gave a shout of delight.

"Of course! How clever of you, David! And if you sail on to some other destination, no one need connect you with the statue when by some lucky chance we uncover it."

"That is what I would hope, sir, but you will have to be very careful that people do not connect the finding of the statue with my visit to you here."

King George was thinking and there was silence for some minutes before he remarked,

"There is always digging activity on Delos to see if anything was left behind by the thieves and brigands who destroyed the beautiful Temples, but they could not destroy Apollo himself."

"I am sure of that, sir, and he is still alive in the minds of anyone like myself, who has been lucky enough to visit the glories of Greece."

King George smiled at the Duke.

"I doubt if any of my subjects go to bed without saying a prayer to the God of Light."

"Then, as I have brought him here safe and sound, and according to Her Majesty only a little injured in one leg, you will require a Temple in which to worship him."

"Strangely enough there is a Temple already under construction," the King pointed out. "And now that you have come here with the God in whose honour it is being erected, I can only think that a mind greater than ours has planned that all this should happen."

He spoke quite simply.

The Duke thought that like the people over whom he reigned he had a respect and love for their Gods that was impossible to put into words.

"Now what I suggest," the Duke said as the King was silent, "is that I spend only a very short time here with you, just a passing visit so to speak. I will then announce that I am on my way to Constantinople."

The King nodded.

"What I must do and the plan now seems to be coming into my mind – is dig a hole for the statue and you must tell me where I can hide it."

He saw the King's eyes light up as he continued,

"When I have sailed away, you can find it quite by accident, or better, someone you can trust will do so, and your people will see it as a miracle."

"They certainly will, David, and, of course, you are quite right. This is a simple way of making sure that Her Majesty is not in any way involved in its discovery."

"What we have to guard against," the Duke added, "is that someone who is not one of your own people finds it first."

"I was thinking of that," the King replied, "and we cannot stop people visiting the island because it is Apollo's birthplace. People from all over the world are anxious, if they are in the vicinity, to set foot on Delos."

"You must tell me where I can lay the God. But Your Majesty is aware that no one, not even Queen Olga, should know that I have brought anything with me but my good wishes."

King George laughed.

"I don't think that any man could receive such a magnificent and unique gift and be able to keep the news to himself."

"But you must try very hard. You know, as well as I do, that if one whisper reaches England that I was in the area, there are always people who put two and two together and make it five!"

65

"Of course I realise that, David, and I swear to you that I will be very careful, and Olga will be told nothing until the statue is actually found. What I am trying to think is where you can put it and where it will be safe until it is discovered as if accidentally."

The two men talked on until it was luncheon time.

The Duke went to the private drawing room that the King and Queen used when they were alone.

It was not even the dining room on the first floor, but a corner room in the Queen's apartments looking East and West with a view of the gardens.

The luncheon table was laid in the window and as a rule it was only for the King and Queen.

However, the Duke learnt that occasionally a Lady-in-Waiting was invited, but very seldom were there any male guests.

The footmen were in Greek national costume and, as the Duke entered, Queen Olga came in by another door.

She gave a cry of surprise when she saw the Duke.

"No one told me that you were here, David, and it is so lovely to see you again."

"And I am delighted to see you, ma'am."

She was looking exceedingly pretty and he thought, as he had indeed thought before, that King George was very lucky to have such a beautiful and charming wife with whom he was quite obviously deeply in love.

They sat down with the Queen asking questions about England and rather curious as to where the Duke was going.

"Constantinople to begin with, ma'am," he replied. "And after that I am not quite certain."

"It is sure to be somewhere exciting and different from where you have ever been before," the Queen said.

"But we did not expect to see you here in the middle of the London Season."

The Duke was making excuses for leaving all the gaiety of London when the meal began with *hors d'oeuvres* and fresh butter and cheese from Tatoi.

The King, he noticed, ate only rye bread and he had heard before that it was impossible to obtain this homely bread in Athens, as the Greeks ate nothing but white bread.

However, His Majesty was not deprived, as a baker on a Danish warship made excellent rye bread and a loaf of it was sent every day to the Palace and in return the King sent a case of Greek wine for the Officers.

After the *hors d'oeuvres*, there were two or three light French dishes, then fruit and desert.

Wine, both red and white was offered to the Duke, but he was aware that it was seldom that the King took a glass.

Instead he drank a whole bottle of mineral water and a cup of coffee which the Queen also enjoyed.

The conversation was mostly on the developments that the King was organising in Greece.

"I can see already that there are many more roads than when I was last here," the Duke commented.

The King, lighting a cigarette, gave a laugh.

"It has been one of the most difficult things to do, but I am glad to say that we can now go quite a long way into the country by carriage. When I first came here, it was only on horseback or flat feet!"

"Everyone in England is impressed by all you have achieved," the Duke said. "And I am convinced that in a very short time you will find yourself having to cope with an enormous number of tourists."

The King gave a groan, but the Queen piped up,

"We will be very glad to welcome them. They will bring money to Greece and that is a commodity we are still rather short of."

They talked and laughed until the King said he had something to show the Duke in his private sitting room, whilst the Queen added that there were people waiting to tell her their difficulties.

"You are not to tire yourself out, darling," the King cautioned her before he left her.

The way he spoke and the warm expression in his eyes told the Duke without words that he was very much in love with his wife.

When she responded by touching his cheek lightly with her hand and looking up at him in an adoring manner, the Duke could tell that they were undoubtedly one of the happiest couples he could possibly imagine.

It passed through his mind that perhaps one day he would feel the same about someone.

Then he told himself that it was a supreme blessing that happened only to those who were very privileged.

If he had married any of the women who wanted to marry him, neither he nor they would now be feeling the same way about each other.

When they went to the King's private sitting room, the King closed the door and announced proudly,

"I have solved our problem, David. It came to me over luncheon, and I know now where you can deposit the statue. I will draw a map to show you where the place is and I don't think you will have any difficulty in finding it."

He took a sheet of paper from a drawer and picked up his pen.

He drew a plan of the Island of Delos and showed the Duke where the new Temple was being built.

"The men working on it are naturally sleeping in tents on the island. It would be a mistake for them to see your yacht anywhere near them."

The Duke nodded to show that he understood, as the King went on,

"Behind the Temple there is a small space where it is planned to fly the flag of Greece or maybe some symbol of the God that will be seen by all those who pass by the island.

"I remember when I first explored Delos and later chose that particular spot to build the Temple on, that there is a small bay directly behind it where there is a cave."

The Duke was now listening intently.

"I was curious enough," the King continued, "to look into the cave which goes back some way into the face of the cliff. I was somewhat surprised to find that it was in good condition and fortunately the winter storms had not affected it in any way."

"What you are suggesting, sir, is that I should put the statue of Apollo into this cave."

"You will find rocks inside you can rest it on and it would be best if it is not wrapped, but just left there as if it has been there over the ages and no one had been aware of it."

"I understand all that Your Majesty is saying, but it would not be wise to leave the statue there for long."

"I will certainly not do so and if you leave it there tonight, I will pay a visit tomorrow to the island, as I often do, to see how the work on the Temple is progressing."

He hesitated as if he was thinking it all out.

"Perhaps I will have had a strange dream the night before that an artefact of great importance is in the cave – "

The Duke remembered that Greek people were very superstitious and a dream was always of great significance whether it was a good or bad one.

"I think, sir, that is a very clever idea," he replied. "The only difficulty is that I must not be seen depositing the statue."

"I have been thinking of that, David, and what I am sure would be a wise course would be for you to anchor tonight some distance away, just out of sight of the island. Then row the statue ashore from your yacht."

He thought for a moment before he continued,

"If it is really late, I am quite sure the workers will all be fast asleep. There will be no one to see you except the moon and the stars."

"They could be dangerous if they are too bright."

King George laughed.

"I think we must pray that the Gods will help us. Now that I live in Greece I realise that many strange and wonderful things do often happen here that do not happen in Denmark. So I do believe that they will help us."

The Duke smiled at him.

"I am sure Your Majesty is right. Now I must leave at once ostensibly being anxious to sail to Constantinople as soon as possible and have no wish to stop on the way."

"Come and see us on your way back," the King said. "I am sure by that time the whole of Greece will be thrilled and delighted by the miracle that has occurred.

"Apollo will have come back to us, and the people will not for one moment suspect that you had anything to do with it."

"I sincerely hope not, sir."

The Duke rose to his feet and then remarked,

"There is one thing I must do before I leave Athens and that is go to the top of the Parthenon. I remember when I was here last time I thought the view from the top was the most marvellous I have ever seen. I could not go away without seeing it again."

"Then, of course, that is what you must do, but you understand that it would be a mistake for anyone from the Palace to accompany you."

"Of course it would," the Duke agreed. "And I will make it clear to everyone that this is just a fleeting visit on my way to Constantinople and I hope to have time on my way home to stay longer."

The King smiled at him.

"There is one issue that is worrying me, David."

"What is that, sir?" the Duke enquired.

"I feel I must," the King said, "send Her Majesty something in return for the present she has sent me. It is so stupendous and utterly marvellous that there are no words with which I can express my thanks."

The Duke could understand his sentiment.

At the same time he knew that actually the Queen had not given away anything that was of any use to her.

In fact, as she had admitted, she had not even seen the statue of Apollo unwrapped – she only knew it was there in a remote room in Windsor Castle.

"I think if Your Majesty writes a letter," the Duke said, "and sends it to the Queen today or tomorrow that will be sufficient."

He knew as he spoke that because he was living in Greece, King George had become very generous-minded and it was always part of the Greeks' nature to give if they received.

People in other countries often accepted a present as a matter of course and then did not attempt to repay it in equal value.

"I must think of something very special to send her in return," the King mused. "While I am thinking, go and climb the Parthenon, but come back here for tea. After all

71

there are many more subjects my wife and I want to talk to you about, which were impossible at luncheon while the servants were waiting on us."

The Duke laughed.

No one knew better than he how the gossip that flowed round the *Beau Monde* in London originated from the servants. They listened to what was said in the dining room and inevitably it was passed on to the servants next door.

"Very well, sir," he agreed. "I will now pay my visit to the Parthenon and then return for tea."

"I will order a carriage for you, David, and I hope your legs will not suffer from the climb. It seems higher and harder to me every time I attempt it!"

"I can rest them all the way to Constantinople," the Duke replied. "But it is a perfect day for me to see Greece from the Parthenon and I only wish I could travel as far as I can see."

"I wish you were staying with us much longer," the King sighed. "But I hope you will soon return and I know that you are wise in making this just a fleeting visit."

The carriage was ordered and the King came down to the courtyard where it was waiting for the Duke.

"Take him as far as you can up to the gateway onto the Parthenon," he instructed the driver of the carriage.

"Be careful and come back safely," the King said to the Duke "and if you wear yourself out or have a fall, we can always send a stretcher for you!"

"I promise you that will not be necessary, sir!"

The Duke stepped into the carriage and, as the King waved him goodbye, the horses set off down the hill.

*

The Duke was thinking that so far everything had gone according to plan and he was delighted with the way the King had co-operated in finding the right method for him to deliver the statue to the Island of Delos.

He was sure that he and Jenkins could manage to row it ashore and in the darkness they could set it in the cave without anyone spying on them.

He might have to ask Captain Holt to assist them, but it would be better if he could manage it without anyone except Jenkins being involved.

He was certain it would be impossible to give the King anything more important to him than the statue and he had had no idea when he left London that the King was actually building a new Temple for Apollo on Delos.

But he knew by the history of the Island that there had been many Temples erected from time to time only to be violated, torn down or burnt.

Yet the worship of Apollo had remained, just as the Goddess Athena was still worshipped in the Parthenon.

The 'Virgin's Chamber', as it was called, had been built on the site of earlier Temples dedicated to the worship of the virgin Goddess.

The Duke had learnt when he was still at school, that it was under construction for more than nine years and it was built entirely of Pentelic marble.

He had travelled all over the world and never seen anything to equal it.

And he knew for his own satisfaction he could not visit Greece without visiting the Parthenon again.

He had been taught that the design for it was drawn up by the architect Ictinus and Pheidias, the great sculptor of the age, was entrusted with its decoration.

These two geniuses had created a wonder that was unique to Greece and which, the Duke felt, was a perfect home for a Goddess of Olympus.

As he drove down the hill, he was thinking that the Gods were still inspiring individuals and it was hard not to believe in them even now.

Surely in some esoteric manner it must have been the Gods themselves who had told King George to build a new Temple for Apollo on Delos.

And was it the Gods who had whispered to Queen Victoria that the statue that had lain hidden for so long in a back room at Windsor Castle was now wanted desperately in Greece?

It all seemed to the Duke to fit in so well with the stories that he had loved reading as a boy.

Perhaps now it was his interest in the Gods that had made him feel that no woman he had met was the perfect female he desired for his wife.

He wished he had time to go to Mount Olympus as he believed that, if he was to sit there in the sunshine and pray, the Gods would help him in his own life.

He hoped and prayed that one day he would be as happy as it was abundantly obvious that King George and Queen Olga were.

He had not missed the gentle and loving way she spoke to him at luncheon and he knew without being told that she was always thinking of her husband and giving him, if she could, everything he desired.

Equally he realised that no one could have played a better part than she had in their joint conquest of Greece.

Not by force, but by love and understanding.

The Greek people were warm-hearted yet idealistic, when it came to those who ruled over them.

They had found Queen Olga exactly the Queen they needed, as she cared for the people and the people cared for her.

The Greeks loved and honoured their Queen Olga and the Duke had learned that there was a special day when their affection reached its highest point.

That was July 22nd in the year that followed their marriage.

It was on that day that the thundering salutes from the guns of the Capital and from the warships in the Gulf of Salamis proclaimed that the succession was assured.

A Crown Prince had been born.

Now at last, after waiting for so long, the Greeks possessed a Prince born in Greece, who would one day be their first truly Greek King for many centuries.

He would be a Greek by birth, by religion and by education.

When the Duke thought about it, he found himself envying King George.

His happiness which came from his wife and infant son was what every man really desired in his heart, but was not often privileged to find.

It was obvious that the two of them talked together, laughed together and ruled together.

That, the Duke thought, was what he really wanted, although he had not until now actually put it into words.

In saying he would not marry, he was trying to save himself from a great disappointment, as nothing could be worse than to find that his love for his wife and hers for him had vanished.

Even if they had children, it would be nothing but a misery and a resentment that he had lost their sublime love that the Greeks understood better than any people in the world.

The Duke looked at the men and women he was passing on the road.

He thought perhaps each one of them was happy because, as well as being very devout Christians, they lived under the protection and inspiration of their ancient Gods.

'Is it what I would find if I married a Greek girl?' the Duke asked himself and then he laughed because he knew he was assuming two much.

Yet whatever nationality his wife was, it was the deep love that the Greeks felt that he wanted to feel for her and her to feel for him.

He could hardly imagine that what he was thinking would not be understood by any of the Englishwomen who had begged him to make them his wife.

At the back of his mind, he had always known that what he really craved was a love that came not only from the heart, but from something higher and more glorious.

'Perhaps it will never ever happen to me,' the Duke thought again.

Then he saw the Parthenon looming up in front of him and it was a shrine that had inspired the hearts and souls of the people of Greece for countless generations.

Perhaps, just as the Parthenon had suffered many vicissitudes in the course of its history, so maybe he had to go through many strange changes of fortune before he too found his heart's desire.

The Parthenon over the centuries had been not only a centre of worship but a National treasury. It held gold as well as priceless ornaments.

It stood as a symbol of Athenian imperialistic pride and the treasure house of Athenian democracy and yet as history progressed, the Parthenon was transformed.

In the Christian era it became a Church dedicated to the Holy Virgin and it was later converted into a Turkish mosque with a minaret attached.

Finally, it became the main ammunition dump on the citadel defended by the Ottoman Turks against the Venetians.

Yet despite all these changes it had remained secure in the hearts of the Greeks.

The carriage came to a standstill.

As it did so, the Duke knew that one day, perhaps even by climbing up to the very top of the Parthenon, he would find all that he was seeking.

CHAPTER FIVE

The climb up to the Parthenon was more exhausting than the Duke could remember, unless, of course, it was because he was now a few years older.

Anyway, now he was there he enjoyed a glimpse of the sun streaming through the many white columns.

He ploughed on, realising that he was now the only person inside the Temple.

When he had entered the Parthenon, there had been a few tourists about, but not the crowd he had somehow expected.

He supposed that the King was right when he had said last night at dinner that there was still a great deal to be done in Athens and it might be a year or more before it was really attractive to modern tourists as other countries were.

"You have done so much already," the Duke had said. "They should be grateful they can at least sleep in a hotel which is comfortable when they leave their ship."

"We need more hotels," the King had replied, "and also more carriages to convey people from one place to another."

Queen Olga had smiled at him.

"You are always impatient, darling," she sighed. "But you know as well as I do that you have done wonders in the short time you have been on the throne."

The King looked pleased and she added,

"Your predecessor did nothing."

"That is what I have always heard," the Duke had chipped in. "And I really do congratulate Your Majesty that you have been able to achieve so much in so short a time."

"But there is so much more that has to be done," the King groaned.

"And we are young enough to have plenty of time in front of us," the Queen had added encouragingly.

"And two successors in waiting for the throne, if I die of exhaustion!" the King smiled.

The Duke laughed.

"If you die then, as we are the same age, I will have to die too! But frankly I have a great deal more of the world to see and discover more challenges to amuse myself with than I have experienced already."

"You are so right, David. George is only wanting us to make a fuss of him. When he tells me he is dying of overwork, I know he really enjoys the power it gives him and he is always full of new and creative ideas."

The Queen spoke the last words almost caressingly and her eyes told the Duke just how much she admired and respected her husband.

Aloud the Duke said,

"I have never congratulated you on your second son when he was born last year. You have certainly made the succession secure and that I am sure is what the Greek people yearn for."

"Baby George, as we call him, is so very strong and healthy that I am quite certain, when and if the time comes, he will make an excellent King."

"As he is only a year younger than Constantine," the King asserted, "I think you are making assumptions that the throne will ever be his."

"We want to make quite sure of the succession. I hope we have a dozen more sons so that Greece will never again have to seek a King from another country."

The King looked towards the Duke.

"I am so grateful," he said, "to be here. I love the people I reign over and I am not being conceited when I say they love us."

"Of course they do," the Duke answered. "I think that they are extremely lucky to have such a charming and attractive Royal Family."

"That is exactly what I wanted to hear you say," Queen Olga exclaimed. "And when you come back for tea you must see Constantine and George. I know they will both be delighted to meet you."

As Constantine was only two years old and George just one, the Duke thought that this was unlikely.

At the same time he could not help himself envying the King a little.

If he had a wife who was devoted to him as the Queen was to King George, then he too would want a family to fill his nurseries and later to ride his horses.

*

He was thinking of all this when at last he reached the top of the Parthenon.

When he stepped out, the sunshine was so brilliant that for a moment he could hardly see his way.

At first, the Duke had thought the place was empty except for himself.

Then he saw at the far end where he intended to go to admire the view towards the Gulf of Corinth and the Aegean Islands, there was one other person.

He moved slowly towards the place where he had stood before and had admired, as he had told the Queen, the most stunning view in the whole world.

Now he was aware that there was another person in the Parthenon besides himself – a very young girl.

She was so small and slight that for a moment he thought she was only a child and should not be there alone.

Then he could see that the girl, actually standing on the very edge of the parapet, was in fact a young woman.

Her long auburn hair was tied up at the back of her head.

She was very slim, and her waist, the Duke thought, could be encompassed by his two hands.

As he walked nearer to her, he realised that she was standing on the very edge in a very careless and dangerous manner.

The drop on this side of the Parthenon was directly onto the ground many hundreds of feet below.

Yet this girl was standing with only an inch or two between her feet and the chasm below.

'I must tell her,' the Duke said to himself, 'that it is dangerous, even thought there is no wind, to go so close to the edge.'

He moved slowly, because the surface was dotted with stones, towards her.

When he had almost reached her, he could see the side of her face and then he realised that her eyes were shut.

He knew instinctively, although he did not know why, that she was praying.

Almost as if someone was speaking directly to him, he realised that she intended to kill herself.

It all seemed to flash instantly into his mind.

She had not moved since he had walked towards her.

Then she went to take one step forward and fall hundreds of feet onto the rocky ground below.

For a moment he thought that he must be imagining such a tragedy.

Yet he remembered hearing that people had died before by throwing themselves from the Parthenon and at the time he had been only vaguely interested.

He realised now, especially in anyone so young, it would be a dreadful and wasteful thing to do.

He drew nearer still.

He saw that the girl was still praying.

Then she flung out her arms as if to spread them before she jumped.

Instinctively, without thinking that it was not his business, the Duke sprang forward.

Seizing her round the waist, he pulled her down from the parapet.

She gave a little scream as he did so.

Then, as he tightened his grasp, she cried out,

"Don't stop me – *I have to do it*. I have to!"

"How could you do anything so wicked," the Duke asked, "as to kill yourself when you are so young and there is so much of your life in front of you?"

"I have to. You don't understand," she protested.

The Duke looked down at her and realised that she was extremely pretty, in fact, *beautiful* was the right word.

Her long auburn hair had golden tints in it and it seemed to be a perfect frame for her large eyes and clear white shin.

"Let me go! *Please* let me go!" she pleaded.

The Duke merely tightened his grasp on her wrist.

"Can you really want to die?" he demanded. "Why, why must you leave this world when you have not lived in it very long?"

"I have to. I have to," she cried out again. "It is the only way I can escape."

"Escape from what?" the Duke enquired softly.

He moved a few steps backwards so that they were no longer close to the parapet and, as he had not loosened his grip on her wrist, she was forced to follow him.

She looked up at him and he saw that her eyes were the deep blue of the Mediterranean.

"Please let me go," she begged him. "You don't understand – I cannot face the future. If I was with my Mama and Papa – I know that they would agree with me."

They were speaking Greek, but her voice was very soft.

Then the Duke asked her quietly,

"Tell me why you wish to do anything that to me is such a wicked waste and I will let you go."

The girl gave a little sob.

The Duke realised that there were large blocks of stone to sit on just behind him.

He sat down on one still holding onto her wrist and she had to sit beside him.

"Now tell me," he urged her, "why anyone so pretty and so young as you should want to leave this world when the sun is shining. I feel certain that the Gods are looking down at you disapprovingly."

He added the last words because he thought they were appropriate.

Once again the girl gave a little sob.

"Perhaps like you – they will think it wicked," she admitted almost beneath her breath. "In which case I will be born again – in a worse position than I am in now."

The Duke knew that she was talking of *The Wheel of Rebirth*, in which a very large part of the world believed.

He therefore questioned her,

"You have been given a very pretty, or should I say lovely body, so what has gone wrong."

"Everything, *everything*!" the girl screamed.

"Suppose you tell me about it. If I release you, will you give me your word of honour you will not make a run for the parapet?"

There was silence for a moment and then the girl answered,

"I promise you I will tell you first and then you will appreciate why I must die."

Slowly, because he was afraid to do so, the Duke took his hand from her wrist.

She rubbed vigorously where he had held her.

Then the Duke quizzed her,

"Now suppose you tell me your name. It will make it easier for us to talk. Mine is David."

"Mine is Thalia."

The Duke smiled.

"A very lovely name and I expect you realise that I am English."

"I thought you looked large and so different from the Greek men."

"Now that we have introduced ourselves, tell me, Thalia, why you wish on this beautiful sunlit day to leave us and go away for ever."

He thought as he looked at her what an attractive profile she had.

It was almost classical and he could imagine her being one of the Greek Goddesses.

"I am being forced," Thalia said after what seemed a very long silence, "to marry a man – I hate and despise."

"Why should you be forced to marry him?"

Again she said nothing until almost as if she felt she had no alternative, Thalia replied,

"If I tell you the whole truth and nothing but the truth, will you promise that, if you cannot help me, you will let me go?"

"Do you mean to kill yourself?" the Duke enquired.

She nodded.

"I cannot imagine any problem, Thalia, for which there is not a solution of some sort. Tell me the truth and I am quite certain I will be able to help you."

"No one can ever do that," Thalia asserted and once again there were tears in her eyes.

"At least give me a sporting chance," he replied. "I have a feeling, although I could be wrong, that you can speak English. I suggest we talk in my language rather than yours."

"Why do you think I can speak English?" Thalia asked him in Greek.

"Your Greek is so perfect that you must have had a good education. I have only to look at you to see that you are what the English would call 'a lady'."

Almost despite herself, Thalia smiled.

"I am glad you think that of me and I must retort by saying you are clearly an English gentleman."

"You are quite right, Thalia, perhaps it would make it easier if I told you that my full name is the Duke of Sherbourne."

Just for a moment her eyes widened.

And then she murmured,

"So you are a very important man and it would be a mistake for you – to concern yourself with me."

"If I am, as you say, important, that is all the more reason why I cannot allow anyone so beautiful to destroy herself. I therefore feel obliged, because, as you say I am an English gentleman, to save you from yourself just as I should save you if you were being assaulted or abducted by ruffians."

"That is exactly what is happening to me – "

The Duke raised his eyebrows.

"I will tell you the truth and then perhaps you will understand. I am actually Princess Thalia, the daughter of Prince Spyros, who was a relation of the previous King Otho."

The Duke was amazed, but he managed to prevent himself from showing it.

"My mother is dead and so is my father," Thalia went on. "But my uncle who I live with is very ambitious that we should be powerful again in this country."

She sighed.

"But the present King is not impressed with him. Although he made various efforts to be accepted at Court, the King has more or less ignored him."

"Why should this affect you?" the Duke asked.

He was thinking she was so very lovely and there must be a great number of men ready to take her out or to flirt with her, if that was what she desired.

"My uncle insists that it would be advantageous for me and for the whole family if I marry Prince Federovski."

The Duke looked surprised.

Then before he could ask the question that was on the tip of his tongue, she continued,

"He is a Russian and I don't like the Russians. He is a particularly horrible and beastly man."

"In what way?" the Duke asked her quietly.

"He is well over sixty. Yet he now wants to have a family that he did not have with his two previous wives, both of whom are dead."

"And you don't want to be the third," the Duke murmured as if to himself.

"Of course I don't!" she exclaimed. "I cannot bear him to touch me and I would rather die than be his wife."

The Duke did not speak and she added,

"Now you understand! How can I possibly marry a man who makes me shudder – every time he comes near me and – who is cruel and horrible. I cannot actually tell you how I know that – but I do."

She spoke violently and the words came jerkily from her lips.

The Duke could tell that every nerve in her body shrank at the idea of marriage to such a man and he could begin to understand now why she was escaping in the only way that seemed available to her.

As he did not speak, Thalia added,

"Now perhaps you understand. So please go away and leave me alone. I will pray as I was praying before you stopped me that wherever I am going my father and mother will be waiting for me with open arms."

"I think they would be much happier if you lived and that is what I am going to insist you do."

"*Insist?*" Thalia asked questioningly.

"I will insist until you have tried my solution to your problem. Which is that we will go now and have tea with the King and Queen at the Royal Palace."

She looked at him in astonishment as he continued,

"I am their guest and I know that the Queen if no one else will totally understand what you feel and she will do everything in her power to help you. So trust me and come with me now and we will tell them what a terrible position you are in."

"You are quite certain that they will want to help me?" she asked. "Even if they do, I doubt if my uncle will listen to them. He is quite certain that, if I marry Prince Federovski, I will automatically be of greater significance in Russia than I am here and he will then benefit by being my uncle."

"What you are saying is that Prince Federovski, whom he wants you to marry, is rich and influential in his own country."

"I believe so," Thalia replied. "That is what he tells us. But naturally even if he is hung with gold and owns half the world, I still hate him as a man."

She paused for a moment before she added,

"I swear to you I could never, never let him be my husband."

She spoke in a way that told the Duke how much it meant to her and then he remarked,

"Prince Federovski, I assure you, is not the only man in the world. Come back with me now to the Palace and I am sure that the King and Queen will look after you. In fact, I feel certain that they will make your uncle see sense."

He rose as he spoke and, taking Thalia by the hand, he drew her to her feet.

"I just want to look again at the wonderful view," he said. "That is why I came here and I think it is the most beautiful vista I have seen anywhere in the whole world."

He led her to the end of the Parthenon where he had first encountered her.

He did not look at her, but he was sure that she was looking in the direction of Mount Olympus and he felt that she was praying to the Gods for help and guidance.

Then he turned round and walked back the way he had come.

"I climbed all the way up these steps," he said, "and I found it hard going, but it will certainly be easier for us going down."

"I thought I would go down more quickly – and in a different way," Thalia muttered beneath her breath.

"It is something you must promise me that you will never even think about again."

As they were now about to leave the Parthenon, he stopped.

"Look at me," he suggested, "and listen to me."

She did as he told her, gazing up at him.

He thought she was even more beautiful than she had been when he had watched her praying.

"Now listen, Thalia. Life is the most valuable asset we possess. We may be rich, we may be poor, we may be like you in great difficulty, but our lives are *sacred*."

Thalia made a murmur, but did not speak.

"It is wrong and wicked," the Duke continued, "to destroy anything so wonderfully made as our bodies and our souls. As we know, our souls have the great privilege of flying up to Heaven above or plunging deep down into the darkness of hell."

As the Duke spoke, he was surprised at himself.

The words seemed to come to him spontaneously, without his even thinking about them.

"It is a gift from the Gods," he went on, "and is life itself. That is why we must never abuse it or deliberately destroy anything so blessed."

Thalia drew in her breath.

"I understand what you are saying and I promise you one thing, I will think very seriously before I try to kill myself again. I will attempt, as you have told me to do, to find a solution to my problem."

"That is all I ask," the Duke smiled. "Now come along. I have seen what I came to see and more important, I have found you."

"I think that is a compliment, but you may wish in the future you had gone away and ignored me."

She did not wait for his reply, but hurried down the stone steps ahead of him.

Because she was so light and obviously athletic, she reached the bottom of the building before the Duke.

As the Duke joined her, she enquired,

"I have come away as you wanted me to. Are you quite certain you really wish to take me to the Palace?"

"We are going for tea and after that I am leaving Athens and I know you will be in hands you can trust."

She did not answer, but walked beside him as they approached his waiting carriage.

The driver was smartly dressed in the Royal Livery and the door of the carriage was decorated with the Royal Coat of Arms.

Thalia glanced at it and then she stepped into the carriage without making any comment.

The Duke climbed in too and, as they drove off, she queried,

"Are you wise in asking me to meet the King and Queen? My uncle has been somewhat rude to them. As I have told you, he is very anxious to regain power in the country."

"He is obviously not going the right way about it, and to force you to marry a man who is old enough to be your grandfather is appalling."

"That is what I told him and I think my uncle has already made himself most unpleasant by disapproving of another King being chosen from abroad, rather than finding a relation of King Otho, such as himself."

The Duke could understand that this was something that might have been considered and yet he was certain that all the relations of King Otho had been deliberately ignored by the Greeks after they had deposed him as their King.

That was why the Princess's uncle was not now of any standing in the country.

He remembered vaguely, when he thought about it, that Otho had married Princess Amalia of Oldenburg and she had made herself very unpopular by interfering with the Government.

From what Thalia had said to him about her uncle it was likely that he had tried to do the same, which was why the Greek people had spurned him ever since King George had come to the throne.

It did not take long for the carriage to carry them to the Palace and the Duke noticed that Thalia was feeling shy and nervous.

"What I am going to suggest," he said, "is that you wait for a few minutes in one of the drawing rooms while I talk to the King, and, I hope, to the Queen. Don't be afraid and promise me you will not run away – "

There was a little pause before the Princess replied,

"I promise you, but you understand that if they say they will have nothing to do with me, I will not return to my uncle and his Russian friend – and I may want to go back to the Parthenon."

"I should be very upset and angry if you did that. So promise me you will wait until I come back to you."

"I promise – "

Thalia looked up at the Duke.

He thought there was something almost pathetic about her.

She was so small and at the same time so beautiful and defenceless.

Yet he knew, although she was behaving perfectly, that she was very frightened.

"I will not be long, Thalia, so please be good and keep your word to me until I come back to you."

She gave him a smile that he thought cost an effort, but it seemed to illuminate her little face.

Then he left her in the room.

He went to look for the King and the Queen and he found them both in the King's study.

They were examining some papers while they sat on a sofa together and the King had his arm around his wife's shoulder, cuddling up against him.

They did not move as the Duke entered.

He thought how lucky King George was to have a wife who made him so happy, yet, as he thought about it, it flashed through his mind that Thalia must be careful what she said about the Queen's countrymen.

"You are back earlier than we expected, David," King George began.

"I have something to tell you," the Duke said sitting down in a chair facing them. "I have found someone who needs your help desperately."

"Who is that?" the Queen asked. "Surely you did not find anyone on the Parthenon."

"That is exactly where I did find her. A beautiful girl was about to throw herself over the edge and end her life. But I have persuaded her to live and have brought her here to the Palace."

Both the King and Queen stared at him.

"Do you mean," the King asked, "that the woman you are talking about was intending to kill herself? We had two people last month who jumped from the top, but they were both suffering from a terrible disease for which the doctors could find no cure."

"What I found there was a very young and beautiful Princess, Thalia Spiros, who tells me that her parents are dead and that her uncle, who is a relative of King Otho, is forcing her to marry someone she does not wish to marry."

The King gave an exclamation, but the Duke went on,

"She was going to destroy herself rather than marry this man who I understand is over sixty years old and has already had two wives."

"*Sixty*!" the Queen cried. "How old is the girl?"

"I did not ask her, but I imagine she is nineteen or twenty."

"Then, of course, it is disgraceful that she should be expected to marry an old man. No wonder the poor girl felt she would rather die."

"That is exactly what she said and I felt sure you would understand, ma'am."

"Did she tell you the name of the man he wanted her to marry?" the King asked.

"She did. He is called Prince Federovski."

Queen Olga gave a little cry.

"Oh, I know him. He is a horrible and disgusting man. He was invited to one of my father's parties in St. Petersburg and behaved abominably. My father swore that he would never invite him again."

"Then you will understand that this young girl is horrified at being forced to become his third wife."

"Of course I do," the Queen agreed. "What have you done with her, David?"

"She is waiting in one of the drawing rooms."

"Then I will go and talk to her at once," the Queen said, "and we will do everything we can to persuade her not to kill herself. Are you sure that is what she was going to do?"

"She was standing on the very edge of the parapet and she protested when I pulled her to safety."

The Queen gave an exclamation and hurried from the room, but the King, however, did not move.

"It is so like you, David," he said, "to be aware of a situation like this long before it reaches my ears."

The Duke chuckled.

"I had no intention of getting involved in anything when I left you, sir, but when I saw this incredibly pretty girl obviously preparing to throw herself off the parapet, there was nothing I could do but prevent it."

"Of course, but you can easily understand that the situation is very difficult, as I have always avoided King Otho's relatives. They naturally resent my taking Otho's place and so have made themselves unpleasant in a great number of ways."

"I suppose that was inevitable. This man who is so anxious to become more powerful in Greece is obviously someone with whom you are not likely to be friendly."

"I have just pretended they are not there. I must be honest and say that after my first year on the throne they more or less accepted the fact that I had won and there was no more argument about it."

"I can well see your difficulty now in helping the Princess, but at the same time she cannot be allowed to kill herself rather than marry that Russian."

"No, of course not," the King agreed. "But now it is teatime. Oh, by the way, I have something I wish you to take back with you."

"What is that?" the Duke asked.

"I have been wondering what present I can give to Queen Victoria," he said, "and I feel it is wrong, when she has been so kind to me, to leave her with an empty space that must have been occupied by the statue of Apollo."

The Duke was about to speak, but then he thought it would be a mistake.

There was no reason for the King to know that the statue of Apollo had never occupied an important place in Windsor Castle or that it had been shut away in a room unpacked where it was never seen.

In fact, as far as the people in Windsor Castle were concerned, it did not even exist.

Instead he asked,

"What have you decided to give Her Majesty, sir?"

"I know well that the British people admire statues and carvings, which is why one of them abducted Apollo in the first place."

They were walking along the passage and the Duke nodded but did not interrupt.

The King went on,

"We have in fact a surplus of statues of Aphrodite, the Goddess of Love. The sculptors of every generation have always tried to make a really perfect statue of her. In my opinion they have usually failed.

The King laughed before he added,

"Like love itself, she is elusive!"

"There I agree with you," the Duke concurred.

"What I have for you to take home," the King said, "is an exceptionally well carved sculpture of the Goddess. They are getting ready to pack it up for you."

"I am sure Her Majesty will be delighted, sir."

He was thinking as he spoke that it would doubtless go into a storeroom and be forgotten, perhaps for a hundred years.

By this time they had reached the drawing room.

As it was empty, the King suggested,

"I expect Olga must have taken the Princess into the room where we are having tea and we will find them there."

It was only a short distance away and the King was right.

The Queen and Princess Thalia were sitting at a table by the window which was loaded with every type of cake, scone and sandwich for tea.

The Princess was introduced to the King and the Duke thought her curtsy was very graceful.

"I know you are in trouble," the King began, "but let us enjoy our tea before we talk about it."

He turned to the Duke,

"I want you, David, to have a look at the Aphrodite statue I have been telling you about before it is packed and put on the carriage that will drive you to your yacht."

"Of course, I am very anxious to see it," the Duke replied politely.

Then the Queen asked him whether he took milk in his tea and the subject was dropped.

In fact tea was quite an entertaining meal.

Thalia told them about the difficulties she had had with her father's family since his death.

The Duke thought it was very astute of her to make it sound amusing rather than miserable, but equally he was aware that she was forcing herself to be brave.

She must have suffered a great deal when she lost both parents and was forced into living with her uncle.

She was, the Duke thought, very tactful in saying little about the Russian monster whom her uncle wanted her to marry.

He felt that few girls of her age would have been so sensitive about the Queen's feelings where Russians were concerned.

She merely complained at how old he was, rather than that she instinctively found him totally repulsive and horrible.

"We will certainly see what we can do for you," the Queen promised.

Then inevitably they talked about the innovations the King had introduced in Athens.

Tea took longer than the Duke had expected and so he glanced out of the window and remarked,

"I think as the afternoon is getting on I should be going back to my yacht."

"Yes, of course," the King agreed. "But I don't expect you will want to go too far before you anchor for the night. As you well know the Aegean Sea can be very unpleasant if a storm suddenly blows up."

"Before you leave us," the Queen added quickly, "you must see the children. I meant to show them to you after luncheon, but actually they had gone to the far end of the garden before you left for the Parthenon. But now they are in the nursery and I do want you to see them both, so that you can tell Queen Victoria about them when you reach home."

"Of course, I will be delighted to meet them."

"Then I will show you and the Princess, if she is interested, the statue of Aphrodite that you are taking back with you to England," the King suggested.

The Duke realised that he was to be very careful not to mention the statue of Apollo while Thalia was there.

It was important that she, like everyone else, should have no idea that the statue of Aphrodite was a 'quid pro quo'.

They walked along the passage and then the King stopped at a door.

"The statue is being packed up here," he said. "So it will be easier to put on your carriage when you leave. I told them to wait until you had seen it before they finally wrapped it up. I don't suppose you will want to undo it again before you reach Windsor Castle."

"No, of course not, sir," the Duke agreed.

They went into the room.

The Duke saw in front of him in the bright sunlight coming through the window a really beautiful statue of the Goddess of Love.

She was kneeling or rather sitting back on her heels and her fingers were pressed together as if in prayer and it was, he thought, about a hundred years old and must have been created by one of the great sculptors of the time.

She certainly looked exquisite and the passing years had damaged her only very slightly.

As a present it was indeed an extremely generous and undoubtedly valuable one.

"It's fabulous, absolutely glorious," Thalia cried.

The King was looking towards the Duke, who after a moment turned and asked,

"Can you really part with it?"

"I would not wish to give Her Majesty anything but the best," the King replied. "But as I told you we have almost a superfluity of this particular Goddess and she will not be missed. I like to think of her beautifying Windsor Castle."

The Duke sincerely hoped that was what Aphrodite would do, but she might end up being pushed away into what were known as the 'lumber-rooms'!

But he could only repeat again how delighted Her Majesty would be with this superb gift.

"The statue will be well packed, as you can see," the King pointed out.

He indicated a number of blankets on the ground, but they were not as good, the Duke thought, as the red ones he and Jenkins had wrapped over Apollo.

But they were brightly coloured and he knew they were the work of the women of Greece in their cottages.

"I promise you that I will take great care of the Goddess, sir."

The King smiled.

"Now come and see the children or they will have gone to bed," the Queen suggested.

She led the way to the door and the Duke followed.

It was only when they reached the nurseries did he realise that Thalia was not with them.

He supposed she had stayed behind with the King for a further inspection of the Goddess of Love.

'Perhaps she will think of posing for a statue of the Goddess herself,' the Duke thought.

Then he found it impossible to think about anything but the two small children the Queen was showing him so proudly.

Constantine at two was a very attractive little boy and he held out his arms to his mother, pressing his latest toy into her hands.

George was in his nurse's arms and the Duke could see that he was a stalwart child, who would doubtless grow into a tall athletic man like his father.

"You are so lucky to have two such beautiful sons," he complimented the Queen.

She smiled at him.

"You have no idea how proud George is of them or how much fuss the Greeks make of them. They always talk as if Constantine will be on the throne in a few years time and George the year after that!"

"I feel sure that you intend to keep your husband alive until he is at least a hundred!"

"Not quite as old as that," the Queen retorted, "but we do enjoy being here and it is marvellous for him to be able to develop and enrich Greece, which certainly needed it when he first arrived."

"I think His Majesty has been wonderful," the Duke remarked.

"I must show you the swings we have put into the gardens for the children and also a special pool where they can paddle and where they will later be taught to swim."

Because she was so enthusiastic, the Duke did not demur when she took him through the nursery window into the garden.

'After all,' he told himself, 'I am in no hurry and we certainly cannot place the statue of Apollo on Delos until after midnight.'

He therefore appreciated what the Queen called her nursery garden and thought it was very astute of them to make a special place where the children could play without coming to any harm.

"Of course the garden was in a hopeless condition when we came here," the Queen was saying. "George left it entirely in my hands and I must show you the beautiful flowers I have been cultivating in the greenhouses."

There was a great deal of garden to see.

The greenhouses, he had to admit, were growing every sort of orchid known to man.

"I love flowers," the Queen asserted positively. "If I have a daughter, I feel sure she will be as beautiful as these roses."

"If she is as beautiful as Your Majesty," the Duke said gallantly, "no one could ask for more."

The Queen smiled.

"Those are the sort of lovely words George says to me. As you must be aware, we are very very happy."

"You make me extremely envious, ma'am. Perhaps I should pay a visit to Russia to find out if there are any more glamorous unattached beauties who look like you!"

"I am sure there are hundreds, David, and the next time you come to visit us, I will have one or two for your approval!"

"If you are talking of marriage, then I can tell you it is a forbidden subject. I have been nagged by my family for years and I have now definitely said I will not listen to one more dreary conversation that starts and ends with my marriage."

"I can understand what you are feeling. But don't worry, I am sure you will find someone you love, just as George found me and you will live happily ever after too."

"I only hope so, ma'am."

At the same time he was thinking to himself it was something that might never happen to him.

They walked back into the Palace.

As they did so, an equerry came to tell them that the King had had to go into the City.

There was a conference that he had forgotten to attend earlier in the day and they had sent a message to say it was vital that he should be there if only for a short time.

"I was assured that His Majesty would be back in time to change for dinner," the equerry told the Queen.

"And I must leave too," the Duke came in. "What has happened to Princess Thalia?"

"I think she went with His Majesty," the equerry replied. "They were together in the tearoom when I told His Majesty about the message from the City. She must have left while I was coming to find Your Grace."

Then he added to the Queen apologetically,

"I had no idea that Your Majesty would be in the greenhouse. I looked first in the music room."

"I was admiring Her Majesty's flowers," the Duke said. "They are certainly a fantastic collection of orchids. In fact, the best I have ever seen."

"I am very glad you are saying that," the Queen replied. "George always says I am a snob because I want to grow only the most exotic and rare flowers. But I find them so exciting because one sees them so seldom."

"That is the right way to think, ma'am. Will you please look after the Princess Thalia and prevent her from destroying herself? I am very worried in case, after I have gone, she is forced to marry a man who is too old for her and she will then pay a visit to the Parthenon again – "

"Leave it to me, David. I promise you she will not marry anyone she does not love. I can assure you that George will deal very firmly with people like her uncle if they try to make trouble."

"I am sorry not to say goodbye to her, but tell her I hope she will keep her promise."

"I will pass on your message," the Queen agreed.

He climbed into the carriage and, after he had done so, the statue was placed in the boot where it could not be seen.

Now it was in a large packing case and, as the Duke knew, wrapped in blankets.

It would have seemed strange for it to be lying beside him in the front of the carriage or even facing him with its back to the horses.

But it was impossible that anyone should suspect that it was a present to Queen Victoria in gratitude for the statue she had sent to Greece.

When they reached the yacht, the Duke gave orders that the statue should be carried into the cabin next to his.

It was where he had locked up the statue of Apollo and actually he thought it was rather a good idea that there would now be a substitute in this particular cabin.

Otherwise some of the crew might well have been curious as to why the cabin had been locked when there was nothing in it.

As soon as the Duke came aboard, *The Mermaid* began to move.

Then he wondered if Princess Thalia would be safe in the hands of the King and Queen.

But the Queen was so kind and so understanding that the Duke was sure that she would look after the girl and Their Majesties would help her somehow to evade a marriage to the appalling Russian.

'As she is so beautiful,' the Duke thought, 'she is bound to attract many other suitors. If she can avoid being whisked away to Russia, a Prince Charming will appear for her sooner or later.'

He thought that if it seemed safe to do so he might stop for a few hours on his return journey just to see if she was safe.

Then he told himself it was not really his problem.

Although she was uniquely ethereal, in fact one of the most enchanting young women he had ever seen, he would be very stupid to become too involved.

The troubles of a young Greek girl could never be of any particular concern in his life.

'I have enough troubles of my own as it is,' he told himself ruefully.

He was thinking of Lady Evelyn and all the other beautiful females who would be waiting for his return to London.

The Mermaid began to move out to sea.

The Duke told himself the only subject he now had to concentrate on was depositing the statue of Apollo safely into its hiding place on Delos.

And then his mission would be at an end.

He would thus be free to go either to some other fascinating place he had not visited before or to return home.

'I know home is where I ought to go,' he thought. 'At the same time Europe and the East are very alluring!'

CHAPTER SIX

They steamed ahead slowly.

By the time they were nearing the Cyclades Islands the sun was sinking steadily into the dark blue sea.

The stars were beginning to come out overhead.

It was then that the Duke sent for Captain Holt.

He was a middle-aged man who had served him extremely well for the last five years and before that he had been in charge of a friend's yacht.

When the Captain came into the Saloon where the Duke was sitting, he saluted him smartly and ventured,

"You wanted to see me, Your Grace."

"Please sit down, Captain Holt. I have something important to talk to you about."

The Captain obeyed him, looking rather surprised.

The Duke had been thinking over exactly what he would say and so he started by asking,

"Are all your crew English, Captain?"

"I did have on board, if Your Grace remembers, one Frenchman, but he left last year. He wanted to work in his own country and I took on an Englishman in his place and on the whole I think it was a change for the better."

"I am sure it was. I am asking you this, Captain, because I need your help in making sure that no one talks about what we have to do tonight."

"Tonight?" the Captain questioned in astonishment.

"Tonight, when it is dark," the Duke replied, "we are stopping near the Island of Delos."

"I thought we'd have moved on a little further than that, Your Grace."

"I want to anchor at least half a mile from Delos, opposite a point where they are building a new Temple to the God Apollo."

"I think I know exactly where Your Grace means."

"I have something special to leave at the Temple and I want you to help Jenkins and me to deliver it."

The Captain nodded and then waited for the Duke to continue.

"It is absolutely essential, because it is so valuable that no one should find out it is there until, as if by accident it is discovered, and then erected in the Temple."

He thought this was a reasonable explanation and he knew it was when the Captain replied,

"I can see, Your Grace, as there's been such a lot of thieving in the past that you don't want it to happen again."

"I thought that you would understand, Captain, and, of course, when one employs people to work on anything as large as a Temple one cannot be responsible for them all, as His Majesty the King has just pointed out to me."

The Captain was quick-witted and he volunteered,

"What you are saying, Your Grace, is that we're to put something ashore which should not be spoken about until it is actually in its rightful place in the Temple."

"I knew that you would follow me, Captain, and I should be extremely upset if any of our crew discussed the matter, and subsequently the present I am giving to the Temple disappeared."

"I am very certain Your Grace can trust them all," the Captain countered almost indignantly.

"But we must take no risks, Captain. I am planning that you and I and Jenkins will take what we have aboard and place it in a spot known only to His Majesty."

He paused to make sure the Captain was following him.

"So we can then carry on with our voyage without worrying that thieves will manage to steal the object we have left behind on the island."

"I fully appreciate, Your Grace, that it would be a disaster. My lips are sealed and there's no reason why anyone should find out if I take you out in a small rowboat in the middle of the night."

"That is exactly what I thought," the Duke replied. "As what we will be taking with us is quite heavy, it would be impossible for Jenkins and me to manage it alone."

"You know I'm always at Your Grace's service."

"Very well, Captain. Anchor, as I have told you opposite the building site. I suggest that if your crew go to their quarters soon after supper, they will be oblivious by midnight of anything we are doing."

"I can assure Your Grace of that."

"I am very grateful for your help, Captain, and I am sure you have guessed that what is locked in the cabin next to mine is the object Jenkins and I will be taking ashore."

The Captain rose and the Duke suggested,

"I believe it is the birthday of His Majesty the King of Greece about now. I think it would be helpful if the crew drink his health over dinner tonight. You will find I brought, when I was last with you, a variety of drinks that are locked up in the galley cellar."

"Your Grace's very generous and extremely wise. I'll take what I deem to be the best for them and I myself will drink His Majesty's health in a glass of Scotch."

"I thought you might say so," the Duke smiled. "I am sure the whisky is far better than any local brew."

They both laughed.

When the Captain had left him, the Duke thought with satisfaction that it was all going as well as possible.

He enjoyed a delicious dinner by himself.

But he rather regretted there was no one he could talk to about his plan for taking the statue of Apollo ashore.

He knew it would be a grave mistake to leave any packing in the cave and it was essential that they should be very careful not to leave any evidence of their entry.

The waves would take away their footprints and there must be no reason for anyone who found the statue not to think it might have been there for hundreds of years.

*

It was nearly half-past eleven when the Duke and Jenkins unlocked the cabin next door and went inside.

The Duke thought it would be a mistake to take more than one candle as he did not want any light to show through the portholes.

The statue of Apollo in its large box, which had originally contained the ornamental screen he had given to Queen Victoria, was standing in the centre of the cabin.

It did not take long for the Duke and Jenkins to untie the case and they quickly pulled off the blankets the Duke had taken from Windsor Castle.

And then they undid the covers that had been there for a hundred years or more.

When the Duke finally saw the statue of Apollo, he realised how exquisitely it was carved.

It was undoubtedly one of the finest statues of the God that had ever been sculptured.

He had seen enough stone carvings in his life to be reasonably knowledgeable about them and he recognised at once that this had been made by a Master hand.

The sculptor must have felt, as any Greek would, that the figure he was creating would receive the worship of everyone who saw it.

It seemed to him extraordinary that Queen Victoria had never looked at this beautiful piece of work and it had remained unnoticed and forgotten in Windsor Castle for all these years.

Perhaps because both the Duke and Jenkins were somewhat awed by the incredible beauty of the statue, they both worked in complete silence.

Then the Duke looked at his watch and realised that the Captain would be waiting for them.

He picked up the statue by its shoulders and then Jenkins lifted its legs.

As they left the cabin, Jenkins pushed the door to behind them and managed with one hand to turn the key in the lock.

Without speaking and as slowly as they could, they went up on deck.

The Captain was waiting for them.

He hurried ahead and climbed down into the small rowboat that was rocking gently at the side of the yacht.

He held up his hands to grasp the legs of the statue.

When the Duke had been unpacking it, he noticed that one leg was damaged as he had been informed and he thought the damage was so slight that it could easily be restored by an experienced sculptor.

He had to lean down over the side of the yacht to lower the statue for the others to take it from him.

When the Duke clambered down into the rowboat, the statue lay in the stern and the Captain started to row towards the island.

Fortunately, the moon was not full, but it gave just enough light with the help of the stars for them to see their way.

The Duke could only hope that at this time of night there would be no one on a passing ship or standing on the shore observing them.

It did not take long for the Captain to row them to the island and he ran the boat ashore in the small bay.

The Duke was feeling certain that they were now in the place the King had told them to find.

None of them said a word as the Duke and Jenkins stepped ashore.

They very carefully lifted the statue from the boat and laid it on the dry beach.

Then the Duke went ahead with Jenkins and found, as he had hoped, the entrance to the cave.

It was rather smaller than he expected and then he thought that this was a good thing, as it would more likely remain unnoticed.

There was in fact no reason for anyone to come to this particular part of the island, and he remembered that visiting ships anchored at the other side, where the walking was easier and anyway there was no shelter from the waves in this part of the island if it was rough.

The Duke had brought with him the lantern that he always kept in his cabin. He had used it in the past when he had sometimes gone ashore alone at night.

Now, without speaking to Jenkins, he lit the lantern and then, moving a little further into the cave, he lifted the lantern high and saw exactly all that the King had told him he would find.

On either side of the cave, which did not go in very far, there were a number of large rocks.

They did not quite reach the roof of the cave, but left just enough space, he thought, to hold the statue of Apollo invisible to a casual explorer.

Jenkins was watching him and, when the Duke put down his lantern, he knew exactly what to do without any instructions.

Together they went back, lifted the statue very very carefully and carried it into the cave.

They placed it gently on top of the rough rocks and there was then no more than six inches between the statue of Apollo and the roof of the cave.

The Duke was thankful to find that the rocks were dry and so there was no likelihood of the sea flooding in and sweeping the precious statue away.

As he laid Apollo gently down, now back at last on his own land, the Duke experienced a strange feeling.

Something he had never felt before.

He could not explain it.

Yet he seemed conscious of the living presence of the God himself.

What he had carried in was no more than a statue of stone and yet in some miraculous way it had become alive just as Apollo himself was alive – that was the reason his people still worshipped him over so many centuries.

Jenkins had already walked out of the cave to join the Captain by the rowboat.

But the Duke remained.

His hand was still on the statue, as if he felt there was something he should still do for it.

For a moment, the whole air seemed to be full of life itself.

The Duke then felt supremely aware of the other Guardian islands, the Cyclades, wheeling round this one small inscrutable island.

There seemed to be a mysterious quiver coming from the statue itself and he seemed to hear the beating of silver wings in the air.

How long he stood there with his hand resting on the statue, he later had no idea.

He just knew that for the moment he was no longer himself.

He was caught up in the mystery and wonder that had made Apollo live for ever in the hearts of those who worshipped him.

As the Duke now realised, Apollo was still alive on his own island and nothing could ever drive him from it.

The Duke could only have stood in the cave for no more than a few minutes.

But to him it felt as if it had been a hundred years.

Finally, he forced himself to pick up his lantern that had mysteriously gone out, perhaps eclipsed by the lights that shimmered in the air above Apollo.

The Duke now felt as if he had passed through an immense experience and would never be quite the same man again.

Slowly he touched the statue for the last time.

Then he moved out of the cave into the moonlight and just for a second he longed to send the Captain and Jenkins away.

They had pushed the rowboat out into the water and were waiting patiently for him to come aboard.

He wanted to stay on the island.

He wanted to be close to Apollo.

He wanted to understand all that the God had to tell him.

He wanted to feel again that strange mystic thrill.

It was given, he knew, only to those who believed in the Gods and worshipped them.

But, if he was seen on the island, he knew people would talk and perhaps it would be guessed later that he had contributed something unique to the Temple.

He forced himself to step into the rowboat.

Then the Captain, who had been standing in the sea, scrambled aboard and picked up the oars.

It only took him a short time to row them back to *The Mermaid*.

There were no lights in the portholes and the Duke guessed that the seamen were asleep.

He was the first to leave the rowboat and climb up the rope ladder onto the deck.

Still without speaking because the words would not come to his lips, he walked down the companionway to his cabin.

He reached it still in the same haze of feelings that he had experienced on Delos.

Then he remembered, just as he was about to open his bedroom door, that they had left the other cabin in a mess.

It would be a mistake if by any chance one of the Stewards opened the door tomorrow and he would see that something had been taken out of the large case that had been brought aboard in London.

'I must put the blankets back into it,' he thought, 'and shut it up.'

He opened the door and now for the first time he realised that his lantern was still in his hand.

He then lit it again and could see in its light that the cabin had indeed been left in a real mess.

He closed the door behind him and put the lantern on the dressing table.

As he did so, he became aware that the packing case containing the statue of Aphrodite that had been in the corner had fallen over and was lying on its side.

He wondered why it had fallen and he hoped that the exquisitely carved Goddess he had to present to Queen Victoria had not in any way been damaged.

So he bent down and tried to pull the packing case back into place.

It was, he thought, heavier than he expected, but he managed with some difficulty to stand it up as it had been before.

It was then he thought that he had better look at it in case in falling over the statue had smashed.

It had been in perfect condition when the King gave it to him and it would indeed be incredibly embarrassing if he had to bring it back to Athens to have it repaired, worse still, if it was broken and he had to plead for a replacement.

It was not difficult to undo the packing covering it and he knew that it had been put on in a hurry.

He pulled it open.

It was a relief to see that the coloured blankets still completely covered it.

If nothing else, they would certainly have prevented the head from being broken off and, if he was fortunate, they might have kept it from being damaged in any way.

Slowly the Duke peeled off the covers one by one.

Then, as he lifted the last cover, he was suddenly struck into immobility.

He thought he *must* be dreaming.

Looking at him with frightened eyes was not the head of Aphrodite that he was expecting, but the face of *Princess Thalia*.

For a moment there was complete silence.

The Duke felt that his experience with Apollo must have affected his mind.

Then Thalia stammered in a tremulous voice,

"I am so sorry – I tumbled over – but I fell asleep."

The words came jerkily from her lips.

There was a long pause before the Duke managed to ask,

"What are you doing? Why are you here?"

"You said – you would help me, Your Grace, but – I knew that they would think it best for me – to go back to my uncle."

She gave a sob.

"When His Majesty was called away," she went on, "I knew this was my only chance of escape."

"What have you done with the statue of Aphrodite the King asked me to convey to Queen Victoria?" the Duke demanded.

He had not spoken since they had left Delos and it seemed now as if his voice was that of a stranger.

It did not seem to belong to him.

"I hid it behind the sofa," Thalia answered. "And when they find it, I hope they will not be angry with you."

The Duke thought they might think him extremely rude or perhaps they would not believe the servants when they said they had packed the object they had been ordered to.

They had then found the statue wrapped in coloured blankets waiting for them in the sitting room!

But the Duke knew that the real question he had to answer was what, now that Princess Thalia was with him, he should do with her.

She was still looking at him pleadingly.

After a moment he remarked,

"You could easily have been suffocated and I am sure you felt very cramped."

"I think it will be difficult – for a while to stand on my legs," Thalia replied. "Or are you – perhaps – going to throw me into the sea?"

Unexpectedly, even to himself, the Duke laughed.

"I will not do that, Thalia, but I am astonished and totally flabbergasted to find you here when, as I expect you are only too well aware, I was looking for the beautiful statue of Aphrodite."

"I am very sorry to have impersonated her in such – a way," Thalia replied humbly, "but I knew that I could not escape my uncle – while I remained in Athens and I might not have – the chance of climbing the Parthenon again."

"You promised me you would not do so," the Duke asserted sharply.

Then quite suddenly, he began to chuckle.

"I don't believe it. Just how can it be possible that you were clever enough to stow away on my yacht? And *what* am I to do with you now you are here?"

"You can, of course, push me overboard and – I am not a good swimmer – "

The Duke did not speak and she carried on,

"Or you could stop at the next island – and tell me I must go home on my own."

The Duke thought, looking so amazingly lovely as she did, she would easily find someone who would escort her to anywhere she wished to go.

At the same time she might also be very frightened by any man who found her alone.

"I suppose," he said, "as you have come uninvited onto my yacht, I must be now hospitable and treat you as a welcome guest."

Her eyes lit up and she asked eagerly,

"Would you really do that? May I please stay with you, Your Grace? Oh please, please – don't send me back! If you do, I will have to die rather than marry that horrible ghastly Russian."

"Those are two things you must not do," the Duke said. "I therefore invite you, Your Highness, to join me on my yacht, although I am not, at the moment, quite certain where I am going."

"You will not go back to Greece?" Thalia asked him nervously.

"I did not intend to return quite so soon," the Duke replied. "I suppose you could hide in one of the cabins while I go ashore, but that would be rather frightening as well as boring."

"Please allow me to stay with you until you reach England," Thalia begged. "I had an English Governess at one time. I am sure if I can find her, she will let me stay with her until I find some work I can do."

"And just what would that be?" the Duke asked her cynically.

Thalia shrugged her shoulders.

"I can teach children Greek. I also speak quite a number of other languages. The only difficulty might be that I am a foreigner and the British would not let me in."

The Duke thought the real problem would be that she was far too beautiful to be independent and earn her own living – certainly too enchanting not to be chaperoned when she was alone with him on his yacht.

Aloud he suggested,

"I think that all these problems can wait, at any rate until the morning. What I want to do now is to go to bed."

"Because it was rather stifling being wrapped up in those blankets and shut up without any air," Thalia said, "I am very thirsty."

"I will find you something to drink. Quite frankly, after this extraordinary escapade of yours, I think it should be a glass of champagne!"

He did not wait for her to answer, but walked out of the cabin and up to the Saloon.

As he expected there was a large bottle of unopened champagne in the ice bucket in case he wanted a drink.

Taking the bottle and two glasses he walked below.

He was aware, as he did so, that Jenkins was in his cabin.

He thought perhaps he would be wise in sending his valet to his own room and then he reckoned it would be more difficult in the morning to tell him the truth than it was at this very moment.

He walked into the Master cabin and closed the door behind him as he began,

"I have just discovered, Jenkins, that we have a stowaway on board. She is a Princess who has run away from her relatives because they are forcing her to marry a particularly unpleasant Russian."

Jenkins looked surprised, but did not speak.

"It is a problem," the Duke went on, "you and I will have to face in the morning. But I think it will embarrass her to meet you now, so go to bed and then I will look after myself."

It was typical of Jenkins to listen without saying anything.

After a short pause he said,

"Very good, Your Grace. What time do you wish me to call you?"

"Eight o'clock. And say nothing of our stowaway until we have spoken to her in the morning."

"I understand, Your Grace," Jenkins replied.

He took the bottle of champagne from the Duke and opened it and then without saying another word, he walked from the room closing the door behind him.

The Duke found it amusing.

He had never known Jenkins, at any time, not to be able to cope with a situation however unusual and however dangerous.

Then he went into the cabin next door.

Thalia was standing and, by the light of the lantern, she was looking into the mirror and tidying her hair.

She turned round when the Duke appeared.

"I have tried to make myself look more presentable. But being shut up for so long, I don't feel that I will do you or your fabulous yacht any credit."

"You have not seen the yacht yet, but you will do so tomorrow. So now come to my cabin and have a glass of champagne and then I will find somewhere for you to sleep."

There were naturally several other cabins on board *The Mermaid.*

The Duke just wondered if the beds were made up. Perhaps the Stewards, thinking he would be alone, had left them without sheets.

In which case, he thought, he would have to offer Thalia his own bed.

As if she knew what he was thinking, she followed him into the Master cabin.

"I don't want to be a nuisance, Your Grace. After falling asleep when I was supposed to be a rigid statue of the Goddess, I can sleep anywhere. Even the floor is not too hard!"

"What a bad host you would make me appear," the Duke countered. "You must think of me, not of yourself."

Thalia laughed.

"You are being very kind and very understanding. I was really afraid that you would rage at me and even throw me overboard."

"I may do so tomorrow, but like you I need a glass of champagne. Suppose we now toast each other for being clever enough to survive."

"If anyone has to survive it has to be me," Thalia murmured. "But you have only yourself to blame for what is happening. If you had let me do what I intended to do, when I climbed to the top of the Parthenon, none of this would have happened."

"Think how boring that would have been for you, Thalia. You cannot be at all certain they would welcome you in the next world – if there is one – and it would have upset the sightseers to find your crumpled body lying on the stones at the bottom of the Parthenon."

He saw Thalia give a little shiver.

"Now you have decided, as I told you to do, that life is important. You therefore have to live your life in the future to the very best of your ability, even if at times it is extremely uncomfortable."

"Like pretending to be Aphrodite, Your Grace. My legs are aching and I am not certain that you will not have to carry me about tomorrow."

The Duke knew that she was teasing.

"You are very light, Thalia, and I daresay that I can sling you over my back if I am going to climb a mountain.

Or perhaps you are right and I should drop you into the sea and instruct you to swim home!"

"I don't think you will do either of those things, but I promise you I have no wish to be an encumbrance or to spoil your holiday if that is what this is."

Thalia thought for a moment before continuing,

"If you will put me down at Marseilles on the way home, I expect I can find my way to Paris where I have several friends who were at school with me."

"Do you think you could reach them safely?"

As he asked the question, he was sure that Thalia would get into endless trouble of her own.

She was too exquisite and too unusual not to attract men wherever she was.

He was afraid too, that her school friends would be glad if her visit to them was a short one.

"You are looking very serious," she commented. "Is it because you are thinking I am a nuisance and you want to be rid of me?"

"I was thinking that you would not be particularly welcomed by any of the girls of your own age, for the simple reason that you are far more beautiful than they are likely to be."

Thalia gazed at him,

"Are you really saying that seriously?" she asked.

"Very seriously. That is why tomorrow when we are not tired, we must sit down and think exactly what you can actually do without having to return ignominiously to your uncle."

"You know the answer to that. I am *not* going back to him. Even if you could prevent me from climbing the Parthenon, I will find some other way, although it may not be easy, of disposing of myself."

"You will not do anything of the sort," the Duke replied angrily. "You will be sensible and somehow the Gods will tell us what you will do and where you will go."

"Are you talking seriously, Your Grace? Or are you in reality laughing at the Gods because we, the Greeks, believe in them?"

"I would never laugh at the Gods," the Duke said, "especially Apollo."

He was thinking of all the strange sensations he had felt in the cave.

Then it suddenly struck him that perhaps Apollo himself knew that Thalia was hiding on his yacht.

And he was telling him that it was his duty to look after her.

'How can I possibly do anything else,' he mused, 'when Apollo himself has made sure I will do so?'

Because he was silent, Thalia was looking at him.

Now she said,

"Please let's be sensible for a moment. I promise I will not do anything to upset you, but I cannot and will not return to Athens. I will go anywhere you tell me, but not to Greece."

The Duke held out his hand.

For a moment, she hesitated.

Then she put her hand in his.

"Now just you listen to me, Thalia. I have saved you from doing what was wrong and wicked. So now, I feel you are my responsibility and I must find a solution to your problem. What I want you to do now is to trust me completely and then perhaps we will find the answer."

He felt Thalia's fingers quiver in his.

And then she said,

"Thank you, thank you so very much for being so wonderful. When I saw the statue of Aphrodite waiting to go aboard your yacht, I knew I would be safe only if I was with you."

She paused for a moment before she added,

"I felt as if the Goddess Aphrodite, to whom I have always prayed, was telling me what I should do."

The Duke remembered what Apollo's statue had meant to him.

Perhaps Thalia had the same feeling about Apollo as he had experienced in the cave.

"What we will both do," he suggested "is to follow the advice of Apollo, which I am sure he will give us if we both pray hard enough."

"Do you really believe that?" enquired Thalia.

"Yes, I do believe it. If you had asked me that question when I was in England, I would not have known the answer. But now I am sure it must have been Apollo who told me when I reached the top of the Parthenon that you intended to kill yourself and that I *had* to stop you."

Thalia's eyes widened and she clasped her hands together.

"I am very prepared to believe," he continued, "that, when I took you to the Palace, Apollo told you he was coming here with me and provided you, quite simply, with the packing that was intended for Aphrodite."

Thalia gave a little cry.

"Do you really believe that? If you do, it's the most marvellous thing that has ever happened. My uncle has always laughed at me for believing the Gods were guiding me. He is a Christian and he scorns the ancient Gods of Olympus and is convinced they have misguided the Greek people for many centuries."

"The Gods have not only helped those who live in Greece, but people who live all over the world have reason to be grateful for the part Greece has played in developing our civilisation."

"How can you be English and say such things?" Thalia asked him.

"Perhaps I am well read and that is what I think you are too, Thalia."

"They laughed at me at school because I wanted to learn so much. Not only about my own country but about the whole world. What I long to do, which I thought so impossible, is to travel to all the countries I have read about and see the whole world."

'As I have been lucky enough to do,' the Duke thought to himself.

"But," Thalia went on, "the people round me wish me not to live my own life but to do what they tell me."

There was a note of both bitterness and fear in the way she spoke.

The Duke had not relinquished her hand and now he tightened his fingers.

"I think we both know now that is what we have to do. To explore the world and perhaps give to other people some of the love, beauty and intelligence that comes to us directly from the Gods."

"How can you believe that and be an Englishman?" Thalia challenged him again.

"Who knows, in my last reincarnation, I may have been a Greek. Perhaps, although you are not aware of it, you were an Englishwoman."

Thalia gave a little cry.

"Oh, do let's talk about it! What you say is so exciting and at the same time so unusual. My uncle would never talk about such issues and conversation in his house was always dull and boring."

"That is something mine will never be. Now if you finish your champagne, Thalia, I want you to go to bed. Tomorrow morning we will sort everything out one way or another."

"I will pray all night it may be my way," Thalia sighed, "which is that I can stay with you and listen to you. I am sure that I would learn far more from you than from a hundred books and certainly from anyone else."

"That is the nicest compliment I have ever had," the Duke exclaimed, "and I will try to live up to it."

He was smiling as he rose and walked towards the door.

"Stay here," he said, "while I see if the beds are made up in the cabin next door or whether, as you have suggested, you must sleep on the floor."

"I will sleep anywhere, absolutely anywhere, as long as I don't have to go back to my uncle!" Thalia cried.

The Duke did not answer.

He merely walked out of the cabin and into the one on the opposite side of the passage.

It was a very pleasant cabin and the Duke had made certain that the mattress on every bed in his yacht was soft and comfortable. No one who used them was upset even by the roughest and most violent storm at sea.

To his relief the bed was made up and then, when he turned down the cover, he saw that the pretty sheets and pillowcases were trimmed with lace.

This cabin had always been intended for any lady he brought aboard with him and strangely enough it had been occupied only occasionally.

He had always preferred to be alone when he was at sea, or else accompanied by a gentleman who, like himself, wished to explore the unknown and to meet strange people who were only occasionally mentioned in the guidebooks.

As he glanced round the cabin, he saw it contained every new gadget that he had installed in his own cabin.

He had been told his yacht was not only the fastest afloat but also the most luxurious.

His orders had certainly been carried out and then it passed through his mind that this particular cabin was so well furnished and so attractive that it might have been designed for a special Mayfair beauty.

The curtains over the portholes and the carpets on the floor were the pink loved by the Egyptians and the blue of their scarabs.

Nothing, he reflected, could be a better frame for the beauty of Thalia.

He walked back into his own cabin.

"Come along," he said to her. "I have found you a very comfortable bed and the sooner we both go to sleep the better."

"I would much rather stay talking to you," Thalia replied. "But, as your guest, I will do exactly as I am told. So perhaps you will not then find me as tiresome as you anticipate!"

"I never said that you would be tiresome," the Duke protested. "I look forward very much to talking to you about a great number of issues that I think would interest us both."

"If you do, it will be very fascinating for me, Your Grace. I have been starved, since Mama died, of all the subjects that really interest me. Starvation of the mind, I assure you, is much worse than starvation of the body!"

"Which, of course, you have not experienced."

"On the contrary! When my parents died and my uncle became responsible for me, whenever I did anything of which he disapproved, he locked me up in my room and I was then not allowed any food or drink for twenty-four hours."

The Duke could hardly believe his ears.

"If it was in summer, it was ghastly to be without water. I have always found that when I am frightened or agitated, I feel very thirsty."

"That is why you asked me for a drink tonight," the Duke said. "You are not to be agitated or frightened any more. This is a ship of discovery and it is Apollo who has brought us together. I am sure we will discover something very wonderful on our voyage."

Thalia clasped her hands together.

"Do you really mean that? Oh, thank you, thank you! You are the most fabulous man in the world. No one but me realises that you are a God yourself!"

"I hope you will always continue to think so," the Duke replied. "Goodnight, Thalia. Sleep well and I am sure we will both dream of Apollo."

Thalia stood looking at him.

Then she murmured in a shy little voice,

"Because you are so wonderful and because you are so kind – I know I am dreaming. Please kiss me goodnight before I wake up."

She threw herself against him and the Duke's arms went round her.

But as he kissed her, it was not, as he had kissed other women, on the lips, but gently on one cheek and then the other.

"Now go to bed, Thalia," he repeated.

Before she could reply to him, he walked out of the cabin closing the door behind him.

Because he did not want to try to understand his own thoughts or his own feelings at this moment, he went quickly into his own cabin and locked himself in.

Then he began to undress and he knew that Thalia was right.

This *was* indeed a dream and only Apollo himself could have given it to them.

CHAPTER SEVEN

The Captain moved the yacht as soon as they came aboard to sail quickly away from Delos.

He did not stop until over two hours later in a small uninhabited bay he knew of further up the coast of Greece.

He was certain that there would be no one to see the yacht anchored there the next morning.

The Duke woke early as he always did.

Looking out of the porthole, he could see where the Captain had brought them.

Because he had a book he was interested in reading, he went back to bed and read it rather than going ashore.

He was thinking that Thalia might want him when she awoke and be worried if he was not on the yacht.

Jenkins came to his cabin at eight o'clock.

He then informed the Duke that their guest was now awake and was dressing.

"I've ordered breakfast for eight, Your Grace," he said. "I thought that was what you'd both be wanting."

"I do indeed need a good hearty breakfast after all the excitement of last night!"

Jenkins laughed.

"It were certainly a surprise, Your Grace. I never thinks for a moment that anyone would be travelling in that there case."

"I suppose," the Duke commented, "it is lucky Her Highness was not suffocated."

He dressed quickly.

Then he went into the Saloon to find to his surprise that Thalia was already there.

She looked up at him with questioning eyes as he entered and he knew she was frightened that he might be angry.

He sat down beside her.

As the Stewards were bringing in their breakfast, there was no chance of an intimate conversation.

They had to talk of other matters and of what was happening in Greece and the Duke told her how much he admired the transformation the Queen had achieved in the Palace gardens.

Only when the Stewards had left, did the Duke ask Thalia,

"Now tell me, what do you want to do today?"

"I don't want to be an encumbrance on you, but I would like, if it is possible, to rest my legs. They are still aching from being shut up in such a small space."

The Duke smiled.

"You can only blame yourself. Even so I think you are right. Later this afternoon I will take some exercise myself by walking on the beach."

She did not reply and he went on,

"I have been to this island before. It's very unbuilt on part of the coast, so I am not likely to see anyone who will ask me awkward questions."

"I am afraid of that," Thalia muttered.

The Duke knew that what she was really afraid of was that her uncle and perhaps the Russian Prince would be out looking for her.

To reassure her, he suggested,

"We will stay here for perhaps only one more night. I have now to alter my plans and decide where I should take you."

"I have already proposed, if it is not too far, coming with you as far as France – "

The Duke was quiet for a moment and then he said,

"Are you really prepared to give up what is left of your family and the country that you have always loved? Surely it would be wiser if you had a further talk with your uncle and attempted to persuade him to be reasonable as to whom you should marry."

"It would be hopeless to do so and just a waste of time. And if my uncle catches me now after running away, I am all the more certain that he will force me to marry the hideous Russian."

There was a note of fear in her voice that the Duke knew came from her whole being.

He accepted completely that it would be hopeless to try to persuade her to go back.

If he did, she might once again go to the Parthenon.

"Very well, Thalia. We will rest here just in case anyone is suspicious that you might have stowed away on my yacht, and we will leave early tomorrow morning while it is still dark and, after passing Athens, carry on down the Aegean on the way home."

Thalia gave a little cry.

"Oh, thank you! Thank you! You are so kind and I am very grateful."

There was no doubt of her sincerity.

"Actually it is really what I want to do myself, so don't be too apologetic. I have to go home as there are a great many matters waiting for me when I return."

He was thinking that he would go at once to the country and concentrate on his horses.

If women like Lady Evelyn missed him, they would not know for some time that he was actually home.

They then went on deck and sat looking out at some small offshore islands and the sunshine and the sea made them look very attractive.

The Duke could well understand that the Greeks worshipped light and believed that it came to them from the God Apollo.

They began to talk more generally and, much to his surprise, he found that Thalia was extremely well read.

Although she had not travelled as he had, she knew from her books a great deal about the countries that he had visited. In fact in some cases she knew rather more of their history and religions than he did.

"How can you possibly know all this at your age?" he asked her.

"I was lucky that Papa owned a large library. Also he travelled a great deal and taught me the languages of the different countries he had visited."

She paused as if she was looking back into the past.

"When his friends called to see him," she went on, "he always allowed me to meet them and to talk with them in their own language."

"It is amazing you should know so much."

"Not half as much as I want to," Thalia asserted. "You have been lucky enough to go to the countries I have only read about. What I want more than anything else is to travel."

She was quiet for a moment and then she added,

"I wonder if I could offer my services in some way to an Embassy. They might easily know people who want to employ a Governess or perhaps a secretary, who spoke several languages."

"I should think that's a very good idea," the Duke said, "except for one thing."

"What is that?" Thalia enquired.

"Because you are far too pretty. Any girl of your age, looking as you do, would be bound to get into trouble if she was out on her own without being chaperoned and without, to put it bluntly, a man to look after her."

Thalia gave a little cry.

"If you are suggesting that I should marry Prince Federovski and go to Russia, then I am *not* going to listen to you!"

"Of course not. I was not thinking of him."

He had really been thinking that, if she appeared in a Mayfair ballroom, every man present would want to be her partner.

"The difficulty with girls as pretty as you," he said aloud, "is that they get into trouble whether they mean to or not. One thing I am certain about is that you cannot travel the world alone."

"Then what am I to do? You know I cannot go home and really there is no home left now that Papa and Mama are dead. And you are right in saying my friends who are not well off will not want to keep me with them for long."

"Don't trouble about it today, Thalia. I am sure we will think of a solution. In fact, I promise you I will. So let's talk about China which you want to visit and where I have been only for a very brief time, also about Japan of which I know a great deal."

Thalia gave a cry of joy.

The Duke found illustrated books to show her what he had seen.

In fact, they were so immersed in what they were doing that they were totally surprised when it was time for luncheon.

It was after they had enjoyed a really delicious meal that Thalia pointed out,

"I don't want to bother you, but you do understand if I am to stay long with you on this lovely yacht, which I hope I will do, I must have some clothes."

The Duke put his hand up to his forehead.

"I really am an idiot," he then exclaimed. "I did not think of that. I forgot you have nothing except what you stand up in."

"It's just what I crawled into that case wearing."

"Well, we cannot stop at Athens, nor can you ask for any of your own clothes."

"I know, Your Grace. I hate to be such a pest, but if you would lend me a little money when we reach Italy, I could buy some clothes. I promise I will pay you back, although it may take me some time."

"You are not to worry about anything like that," the Duke said. "I am sure we can stop in Naples where you will find everything you want. Or would you prefer to go on to Marseilles? It will be my present to start you on your new life, the details of which we have not yet decided."

He was thinking as he spoke, although he did not say it aloud, that perhaps he would be wise to take Thalia straight back to England.

He could then find some sensible family living in the country who would welcome anyone so well educated and so good at languages.

But there was one serious difficulty.

If he arrived in England with Thalia and anyone knew that they had been alone in his yacht, her reputation would be ruined and indeed his would be tarnished.

'I will have to cross that bridge when I come to it,' the Duke told himself.

Equally he knew it was a major problem that had to be resolved sooner or later.

*

It was about three o'clock in the afternoon when the Duke announced,

"Now I am going for a walk. I will not be away for long. After dark we will move further down the Aegean Sea. I am sure you will enjoy the beauty of the scenery we will see tomorrow."

"That will be very exciting, Your Grace, and I wish I could walk with you, but to be honest my legs are still rather stiff and I would prevent you from going at anything but a snail's pace."

"You can come with me tomorrow or the next day. You are most sensible to rest you legs while you have the chance. There are a great many books below that I know you would find absorbing. My 'sea-library' as I call it, is really quite up-to-date."

Jenkins had shown her the cabin where his books were arranged to make a small library and she had already told him how clever he had been to think of anything so sensible.

"I have heard people complain over and over again when they have been on a long voyage that they became bored," she said. "The books available on the big liners are, I am told, usually cheap novels I know you would not enjoy."

"I certainly would not," the Duke agreed.

He thought that most women of his acquaintance would prefer novels to history or biography.

It was certainly strange to find in a young girl who was so interested in the history of other countries.

He had put on his most comfortable clothes when he had dressed that morning.

Thus he did not have to change before he swung himself over the side of the yacht and two sailors rowed him the short distance to the beach.

Thalia lent over the rail to watch him go.

When he reached the top of the low cliff above the beach, he turned round and waved before he walked off.

She waved back.

Then she sat down in a shady place on deck to read two of the books he had recommended to her.

Because he rode so much, the Duke found that it was essential to take some exercise when he was at sea.

He was determined to keep as fit as he had always been and so he walked quickly over the short grass.

He then found that the landscape, although devoid of people, was very attractive.

There were wild flowers creating patches of colour in the sunshine and in the trees he passed there were birds singing. Some of them had coloured feathers that made them look as if they had stepped out of a Fairy story.

He had gone quite a long way when he thought he would be wise to return.

Actually, he had found the sun rather hotter than he expected and so he sat down and rested for a little while under some shady trees.

Then he set out, feeling surprised at the distance he had covered.

He was moving rather slowly on his way back as it was so hot.

It must have been almost two hours later that he saw the masts of what he knew must be another ship near to where *The Mermaid* was anchored.

He wondered why there was a ship in this barren and uninhabited part of the country and it seemed to him not only strange but perhaps dangerous.

He quickened his pace.

Even so, he still had a long way to go.

He was feeling very hot when he eventually came near enough to see the mast of *The Mermaid.*

Immediately behind it was the funnel of a much larger ship.

Now he was really worried.

He broke into a trot.

He was almost certain from the markings on the funnel that this ship was Russian.

Before he left he had told the Captain where he was going and he had suggested,

"I think that's a good idea, Your Grace, and as the men are anxious to have a swim, I'm allowing the majority of them to go a little way up the coast."

"I am sure they will enjoy it," the Duke had replied. "I will very likely bathe myself this evening."

"I was thinking just the same, but I thought perhaps Your Grace would want to move on as soon as it is dark."

"We have the whole night to sail away in and if we keep close to the coast, there is little likelihood of anyone on the island noticing us."

The Captain nodded.

But now it seemed as if a Russian ship had already found them.

The Duke was afraid it may contain the man Thalia was so frightened of.

He reached the top of the bay where his yacht was anchored.

As he did so, he saw that the ship, which was only a short distance from her, was undoubtedly Russian.

Then to his relief he saw that the boat he had come ashore in was pulled up on the beach.

Standing beside it was Jenkins.

He hurried down the cliff to his valet's side.

"What is happening, Jenkins?"

"The Ruskies be here, Your Grace, and some of the men be shut up in the Saloon with Her Highness."

"You did not stop them coming aboard?" the Duke asked sharply.

He was dragging the boat, with the help of Jenkins, down the beach and into the water.

"They just walked in, Your Grace, and there were only one Steward on duty. They just pushed him on one side."

As Jenkins was talking, he climbed into the boat and started to row the Duke the short distance to the yacht.

"I sent one of the seamen, Your Grace, to notify the Captain who had gone for a swim and they should be back any time now."

"I sincerely hope so,"

As they reached the side of *The Mermaid*, the Duke then pulled himself up to the deck.

Jenkins left the boat and followed him.

The deck was empty.

As he walked forward, Jenkins pushed something hard and cold into his pocket.

He realised it was a revolver and his fingers closed over it.

The Duke walked on without stopping to the door of the Saloon.

He opened it and entered with Jenkins behind him.

What he saw made him stop just inside the Saloon and draw his breath.

At the far end, Thalia had been gagged and ropes were being tied round her body by two Russians.

Watching them, with for a moment his back to the Duke, was an elderly Russian.

The Duke was sure that he was Prince Federovski.

Two other men were kneeling on the floor, pulling on the ropes and tying Thalia's legs together.

The Duke walked forward.

"And what the hell do you think you are doing?" he demanded in a voice of thunder.

The Russian Prince turned round.

"I am taking back my own property," he replied harshly.

Without really thinking too much about it, the Duke had spoken in Russian – as it so happened he was quite proficient in that language.

"She is not your property and, as the Princess is my guest, you will kindly not insult her as you are doing at this moment."

The Russian sneered at him and there was no other word for it.

At the same time he pulled a revolver out of his pocket.

Before the Duke could draw his, Jenkins, standing behind him, shot the Prince in the shoulder.

He gave out a scream of agony, lost his balance and fell to the floor with a crash.

Then the other Russians started to reach for their weapons.

As they did so, there was a sound of men running across the deck.

A moment later the Captain burst in, followed by eight of his men, all carrying firearms.

Some of them were still in their bathing clothes.

Then there was the sound of even more footsteps following them.

Without being ordered to do so, the Russians put down the guns they had reached for.

"You take His Highness back to his ship," the Duke ordered, "and set off to sea immediately. He requires the attention of a doctor."

As he was speaking to them in their own language, the Russians could not pretend they did not understand.

With a wary glance at the number of seamen facing them, they moved towards the Prince.

He was groaning as he lay on the floor.

Four of the Russians picked him up and carried him out of the Saloon onto the deck.

The Captain followed them and gave instructions as to how to transport the wounded man back to their own ship.

As they left the Saloon, the Duke shut the door and went quickly to Thalia.

He first took the gag from her mouth.

Then he saw that fortunately the Russians had not been very skilful in tying her up.

The ropes fell off easily when he pulled at them.

Then he gently put his arms round her and pulled her out of the chair they had pushed her into.

It was then that Thalia burst into tears and hid her face against his shoulder.

"It is all right, my darling. They will not hurt you now and they will never take you away."

As she went on crying, he picked her up in his arms and carried her to the sofa.

He set her down on it.

Then, kneeling beside her, he wiped the tears away from her eyes with his handkerchief.

As he smoothed her hair back from her forehead, she then looked up at him, her eyes still wet with tears and whispered,

"I prayed and prayed that you would come to me *and you came*."

"I felt that something was wrong. When I saw the masts of the Russian ship, I knew it meant danger."

"They were taking me away and he claimed that he was going to marry me immediately."

"That is something he will never do and I think his wounded shoulder will keep him out of mischief for a long time."

"You came – and you saved me," Thalia muttered again.

She looked so lovely, at the same time so pathetic.

Without really thinking, the Duke bent forward and his lips found hers.

He had not meant it to be anything but a gentle kiss to sweep away her fears.

But when he kissed her, he felt again that strange mystical feeling he had experienced on Delos.

It was the feeling he had subconsciously longed for and knew it belonged to the Gods, *but now it was his*.

He kissed her very tenderly at first.

Then, as he felt her respond, his kisses became more possessive and more passionate.

As he held her closer, her arms went round him.

He knew she was feeling the same as he was. It was an indescribable wonder that could only come from the Gods themselves.

"I love you," the Duke sighed when he could speak.

"And I love you," Thalia answered. "I have known it ever since you saved my life – but I believed that I could never mean anything to you."

"You mean everything I have always searched for and longed for, Thalia, but thought I would never find."

Then he was kissing her again.

Kissing her wildly and determinedly, as if he was afraid he might lose her.

He felt, as he did so, as if he was now at one with the Gods.

He was certain, although he could not put it into words, that there was the whirling of silver wings that he had heard on Delos and which he knew came from Apollo himself.

"I love you. I love you!" he cried again and again.

He felt that when he kissed Thalia they were both carried into a Heaven they had never known before in their own world.

It might have been a thousand years later or perhaps only half-an-hour, when the Saloon door opened and the Captain appeared.

"We have got the Prince on board his ship, Your Grace, and it would be wise if we sailed away at once."

"Yes, yes of course, Captain," the Duke managed to say. "Keep out of sight of the mainland if you can and try to make it impossible for the Russians to follow us."

"I don't think that is their intention, Your Grace, but I never trust the Russians and certainly not those who came here today."

"You are quite right, Captain, and the sooner we are well away from them the better."

Even as he spoke, he heard the engines turn over and they would soon be moving away from the Russian ship.

Then, when the Captain had gone, closing the door behind him, Thalia held out her arms crying,

"Please don't leave me. I will not feel safe until we have left that horrible man behind."

"You are safe with me," the Duke assured her, "and you always will be."

She looked at him enquiringly and he thought that no woman in the whole world could look so lovely or so ethereal.

There was an expression in her eyes he had not seen before.

Her glorious auburn hair, which had been loosened when the Russians had put the gag on her, now fell either side of her cheeks.

It made her look very young and at the same time, the Duke thought, almost like an angel or perhaps the right word would be 'a Goddess'.

"I cannot believe that I have really found you," the Duke sighed. "I was quite certain you did not exist."

"I thought when you prevented me killing myself, you were like an archangel come down from Heaven and the most wonderful man in the world."

"When did you know you loved me, Thalia?"

"I think almost as soon as I first saw you. I was so frightened that you would go away without me that I knew, even if you were angry, I *had* to be with you."

"I can only thank God you did. I must have been crazy, after I had seen you and knew you were the most beautiful woman I had ever seen, to think of leaving you behind."

"And I can stay with you now?" Thalia whispered.

"You can stay with me for ever. I am just trying to think and it is difficult when you are so close to me, where we can be married."

"Do you really want to marry me?" Thalia asked him softly.

"I am going to marry you and keep you with me from now into Eternity," the Duke asserted.

"Oh, it is wonderful, so unbelievably wonderful. I am only afraid it is just a dream and I will wake up."

"It is real, so real that I cannot wait to marry you. I am going to tell the Captain now to turn the yacht round and we are going back to Athens."

Thalia gave a little cry of horror.

"To Athens!" she exclaimed. "But why? Why? They will persuade you to send me back to my uncle."

"No one in the world can ever do that. I have no intention of even letting you see your uncle. What we are going to do, my precious one, and I know it is right, is to be married in the Royal Chapel at the Palace."

Thalia stared at him.

"But will they let you?" she asked.

"I think it would be difficult for them to refuse. I am sure the King will understand when I explain to him why that is what I really want."

"Why do you want that?" she asked in a frightened little voice.

"I am making sure that your uncle does not claim to be your Guardian and therefore by law is entitled to choose a husband for you and marry you off to whom he pleases."

"Yes, he told me he could do just that."

"He might try to make trouble if we run away to be married," the Duke went on. "So, to be certain he cannot, we will be married at once in Greece, your own country, and I am hoping that the King and Queen will be present at the Ceremony."

He paused before he added,

"I am sure, if I ask him to, he will understand why it is essential."

"You are so clever," Thalia exclaimed. "Only you could realise that this would prevent there ever being any dispute about my being your lawful wife."

"I thought you would agree. And the moment the Service is over we will leave for our honeymoon and will not listen to any protests, if there are any."

He smiled at her as he went on,

"The wedding will be announced first in the Greek newspapers, and then in the English, French and German ones as well. I will see to it and afterwards it will be quite impossible for anyone to take you away from me."

Thalia threw her arms round the Duke's neck.

"I love you and I think you are the most fantastic man in the whole world," she murmured happily against his shoulder.

He kissed her.

And then when his lips set her free, she asked,

"How could I have guessed when you pulled me off the parapet that I would ever be your wife? You are so wonderful and marvellous and I will ask myself for the rest of my life how I could have been lucky enough to find you."

"I will be doing the same. I believed you did not exist and that all those stories of looking for 'the other half of oneself' were just people's imagination."

"They are true, really true," Thalia cried. And I know now that it was the Gods who brought us together.

"Just one God and that was Apollo."

He thought as he spoke that it was Apollo who had planted in him these overwhelming feelings of love.

He had imagined that they existed, but had never been certain of it.

Now he knew they were real.

Every single time he kissed and touched Thalia, they would be united by the love that came from Apollo and also, he now thought, from Aphrodite as well.

How was it possible, the Duke wondered, that the statues of the two Gods could have brought them together in such a curious way and at the same time giving them the love that he had never expected to find anywhere in this world.

*

They arrived back in Athens when there was only the moonlight to glitter on the Parthenon.

However, the Duke hoped that the King, if not the Queen, would be awake.

He left Thalia well protected by Jenkins and the Captain and hurried to the Palace.

He was right, neither the King nor the Queen had retired and they were sitting happily together in one of the Palace drawing rooms.

When he entered the room, announced by a servant, the King jumped to his feet.

"What has happened, David?" he asked him. "Why have you come back? Has anything gone wrong?"

"I have something to tell you that I think you will find hard to believe, but you may have guessed already why the Goddess Aphrodite was left behind."

"I am sure that naughty child took her place," the Queen remarked.

"You are quite right," the Duke admitted. "But that child, as you call her, has had a further very unpleasant experience."

He sat down and told them how he had placed the statue of Apollo exactly where the King had told him to put it.

How on returning to *The Mermaid* he had found a stowaway on board and how they had sailed on to anchor out of sight of Delos.

And how the Russian ship had somehow managed to find them.

The Queen gave a cry of horror.

"Oh, that awful man has not taken the poor little Princess away, has he?"

"We saved her from that," the Duke replied. "But now the only way I can make certain he does not try again, is for us to be married at once. If Your Majesties would allow us to be married here in your Palace, there could be no argument about it once the Ceremony has taken place."

For a brief moment, the King and Queen appeared speechless.

And then the King laughed.

"You have never ceased to surprise me, even when we were boys together, David," he said. "But I think she is the most beautiful creature I have ever seen with naturally the exception of my wife. I am not surprised that you want to marry her."

"And she wants to marry me. So we hope we will both be as happy as you are."

"Of course you will be," the Queen added. "And as you say, things being difficult, you had better be married as quickly as possible."

"That is what I want and we would be grateful if we could be married first thing tomorrow morning before there is time for the Russian Prince to get here and try to make trouble."

The King spread out his hands.

"The Palace is at your disposal, my dear David, and Olga and I will be only too delighted to be witnesses at your wedding."

"That is just what I hoped you would say, sir, and I am extremely grateful. After that I will be taking my wife on a honeymoon and then to England. I doubt if her uncle or Prince Federovski can then make any trouble at all."

"It will be quite impossible for them to do so," the King agreed. "I suggest that you have your wedding about nine o'clock."

"That will be marvellous, sir. You will understand if we leave immediately afterwards, just in case her uncle or any of her other relatives turn up to make trouble."

He deliberately did not say any more about the Russians.

"Now I will go back to the yacht and tell Thalia how kind you have been."

The Queen gave a little cry.

"I have just thought of something. Being a man, it has not occurred to you."

"What can it be?" the Duke asked.

"The poor child will obviously only have the dress she was wearing when she crept into the case that should have held Aphrodite."

The Duke waited and the Queen continued,

"Bring Thalia here at eight o'clock and I will dress her as a bride should be."

She smiled at the Duke.

"Of course I will also give her as a wedding present a few dresses of mine to start her honeymoon with until you take her somewhere where there are dress shops."

"You are very kind, ma'am. And of course clothes matter more to a woman than they do to a man."

"Oh, you and George look good in anything, but I am sure that Thalia will want to remember her wedding day and nothing could be worse than if the bride feels she is not looking her very best."

"You have always been most generous, ma'am, and I know how grateful Thalia will be."

The Duke kissed the Queen's hand and then turned to the King,

"Thank you, sir, more than I can ever say."

"I know you would have done the same for me if our positions had been reversed. The only thing I ask in return, David, is that, when your honeymoon is over, you come back here and tell us how happy you are."

The Duke smiled.

"We will certainly do so, sir."

Then he hurried back to *The Mermaid*.

He had given orders that Thalia should have every possible protection.

Yet he was still afraid that something might happen at the last moment to separate them.

*

The following morning the Duke and Thalia went aboard *The Mermaid* after what had been a very moving and incredibly beautiful Service in the Royal Chapel at the Palace.

The King and the Queen were the only witnesses.

The organ was played by someone they could not see and the King's private Chaplain performed the Service with just two acolytes to assist him.

Dressed in the same gown in which Queen Olga herself had been married and wearing her veil, Thalia looked indescribably glorious.

As lovely, the Duke thought, as an angel who had stepped down from Heaven.

The wreath on her head was made of white orchids and so was the bouquet she carried. And the Duke knew that they came from the greenhouses the Queen had had built in the Palace garden.

When the Service was finished, the King and the Duke talked together.

While the Queen helped Thalia to change into a 'going away' dress, there was a hat trimmed with flowers to match it.

She looked ethereal when she came down the stairs to the drawing room.

The King and Queen drank their health.

Then they drove back to the yacht after thanking their Majesties a thousand times for their kindness.

"I assure you it has been very exciting for us too," King George enthused as they waved goodbye. "Olga is jealous of you going on your honeymoon, so I have had to promise her that we will go on another one ourselves at the end of next week!"

He looked very happy about it and both the Duke and Thalia knew that their love was as real as their own.

*

Thalia held the Duke's hand as they drove back to the yacht.

There they saw *The Mermaid* decorated with flags and flowers.

They were not surprised when they went into the Master cabin to find that the Queen had sent a profusion of different flowers for that room as well.

As *The Mermaid* moved slowly out of the harbour, the Duke put his arms round his wife and sighed,

"I love you, Thalia, and now no one can take you away from me. You are mine, not only in this world, but for all Eternity."

"Oh, darling, wonderful David. I am so happy and I feel it cannot be true and I am really back standing on top of the Parthenon waiting to jump and escape for ever from everything that terrified me."

"You will never be frightened again," the Duke said, "and, my precious, now you are mine I can tell you far better than I have been able yet to do, how much you mean to me."

As the yacht moved away from Athens and down the Aegean Sea, the Duke held his wife closer still.

They realised that they were completely alone and no one would disturb them.

Very gently the Duke took off the hat the Queen had given Thalia.

Then he undid the dress that was only slightly too large but very becoming.

As they sank down on the large bed surrounded by flowers that scented the air, Thalia whispered,

"I love you, I love you so much, David. Why are there no other words to express the way I feel for you?"

"It is much easier to say it without words," the Duke replied and his voice was very deep.

As he spoke, he first kissed her lips, her neck, then her breast.

"You are all mine, absolutely and completely mine, my darling Thalia. I was quite certain you did not exist except perhaps in Olympus."

"I was frightened of all men – until I met you."

She was speaking softly.

Her voice was a little shaky because the Duke's kisses were exciting her.

It was in a way she had never been excited before.

She could not explain it, even to herself.

"I love you and I adore you!" she struggled to say between his kisses.

Then, as the Duke made her his, they both knew that it was Apollo who had opened the doors of Heaven for them.

As they passed through, they found the perfect love that could only come from God and the Love that was to be theirs not only in this world but for Eternity and beyond.